The
Karen Connors

PAN HORIZONS

Judy Blume
Forever

Bruce Brooks
The Moves Make the Man

Aidan Chambers
Dance on My Grave

Lois Duncan
The Eyes of Karen Connors
Stranger With My Face
I know What You Did Last Summer

Paula Fox
The Moonlight Man

Merrill Joan Gerber
I'm Kissing As Fast As I Can
Also Known as Sadzia!
The Belly Dancer

Virginia Hamilton
A Little Love

Rhodri Jones
Hillsden Riots

Toeckey Jones
Skindeep

M. E. Kerr
If I Love You, Am I Trapped
  Forever?
Is That You Miss Blue?
Night Kites
The Son of Someone Famous

Norma Klein
Beginner's Love
Breaking Up
It's Not What You Expect
It's Okay If You Don't
  Love Me
Angel Face
Going Backwards

Harry Mazer
I Love You, Stupid
Hey Kid! Does She Love Me?

Richard Peck
Are You In The House Alone?
Remembering The Good Times
Close Enough To Touch

Sandra Scoppettone
Long Time Between Kisses
Happy Endings Are All Alike

Rosemary Wells
When No One Was Looking
The Man In The Woods

Barbara Wersba
Tunes For A Small Harmonica

Patricia Windsor
The Sandman's Eyes
Killing Time

The Eyes of
Karen Connors

Lois Duncan

PAN HORIZONS

First published 1984 by Little, Brown and Company
First published in Great Britain 1985 by
Hamish Hamilton Children's Books
This edition published 1986 by Pan Books Ltd,
Cavaye Place, London SW10 9PG
9 8 7 6
© Lois Duncan 1984
ISBN 0 330 29248 X
Phototypeset by Input Typesetting Ltd, London
Printed and bound in Great Britain by
Hazell Watson & Viney Limited
Member of BPCC plc
Aylesbury, Bucks, England

For my daughter Kate
who has waited so long and so patiently
for a book her very own

1

Bobby Zenner disappeared sometime between noon and one o'clock on the third Saturday in April. Later, under police questioning, Karen would not be able to pinpoint it any more closely than that. She had been babysitting the Zenner children since ten that morning, and Bobby and two of his friends had been tearing around the house like mad things, engaged in one noisy game after another. Finally, around noon, she had sent them outside to run off energy and to allow her some peace in which to give lunch to the baby.

It was while she was spooning Jell-O into the mouth of eighteen-month-old Stephanie that the doorbell rang.

'Oh, honestly! It's not as though I had him locked out,' Karen muttered in exasperation as she took a token swipe at the baby's sticky chin with a food-covered bib.

After checking the safety strap to make sure Stephanie was securely anchored in her high chair, she went into the living room to open the door.

'There's a perfectly good knob—' she began, and broke off abruptly at the sight of the tall, dark-haired young man on the front step. 'Tim! What are you doing here? I thought it was Bobby.'

'I was over at the service station getting a tyre patched, and I remembered you were going to be here today. I thought I'd stop and say hi.' Tim Dietz gave her a familiar, self-assured grin. 'Aren't you going to invite me in?'

'I can't,' Karen said regretfully. 'The Zenners—'

'Don't want strangers in their house?'

'It's one of the ground rules.'

'Am I a stranger?' Tim asked playfully. 'Be honest now.

'To them you are.'

He continued to smile at her. 'What if I give my solemn promise not to rip off any of the silverware?'

The smile was contagious. Karen found herself returning it. With a sigh of defeat, she stepped back from the doorway to allow him to enter.

'OK, but just for a minute. You'll have to come out to the kitchen. I'm in the middle of feeding the baby.'

Once he was inside with the door shoved closed behind him, shyness came sweeping over her. She knew it was ridiculous. She and Tim had been dating steadily since early February. They had been to movies and basketball games and out for pizza and had done some prolonged parking up on Four Mile Hill, which was where most of the high school couples ended their evenings. Tim routinely waited at her school locker to walk her to classes and held a place for her at the Lettermen's Table in the cafeteria. The names 'Tim-and-Karen' were beginning to be linked, even by those who hardly knew her. So why was it, still, that every time they were alone together she couldn't seem to get quite enough air into her lungs?

Hoping Tim wouldn't notice her breathlessness, Karen led the way into the kitchen, where Stephanie was entertaining herself by squeezing Jell-O through the cracks between her fingers. The tray of the high chair held a cherry-coloured pool of melted gelatin, and the bowl which had been its container lay upside down on the floor.

Tim regarded the scene quizzically.

'Who's this charming creature? Does she do this often?'

'She's Stephanie Zenner, and she does it all the time.' Karen detached the tray and carried it over to the sink. 'She's a darling, but you can't turn your back on her.'

'Is the other one this bad?'

'Bobby? He's seven, so he doesn't make the same kind of messes. The problem with him is that he's too old to tie into a chair. He takes off running when he gets up in the morning, and he doesn't stop until he keels over at night.'

'How do you stand it?' Tim asked. 'I'd go nuts.'

'Oh, it's not that bad. I like kids. I work at the Heights Day Care Centre in the summers. I always used to wish I had a brother or sister.' Karen picked up a dish towel and held it under the faucet. 'Once when I was about five, my mother told me I was going to get a baby for Christmas. I was so excited I couldn't sleep that night. On Christmas morning, I went rushing down to look under the tree, and do you know what was sitting there? A *doll*! One of those life-sized baby dolls that drink and wet. I was so disappointed I cried.'

'I'd say you came out ahead on the deal.'

'I didn't think so.'

She wrung out the towel, and went back to the chair to wash off Stephanie. Tim moved to stand behind her, slipping his arms around her waist.

'Your hair smells good. Like flowers.'

'It's a new shampoo,' Karen said inanely. 'It's supposed to give extra body.'

'Your body's good enough for me the way it is.'

Karen drew a shaky breath. 'I'm glad of that, but I don't think you ought to be telling me about it right now. I've got to get Stephanie down for her nap.'

Tim brushed his lips along the back of her neck just below the hairline.

'Turn around,' he demanded huskily.

'Not here, Tim, please. It's not like we were out on a date. The Zenners are paying me—'

'I'm not trying to rape you, for Christ's sake! All I want is a hello kiss.' He raised his hands to her shoulders and turned her so she was facing him. 'What's all this touch-me-not stuff all of a sudden? Are you afraid the kid's going to tattle?'

'Of course not,' Karen said. 'It just makes me nervous to think about making out in somebody else's house. Bobby could come bursting in at any moment.'

'Big deal – so Bobby finds out that his sitter has a boyfriend.' Tim started to pull her against him and then abruptly released her as the dish towel, which had become sandwiched between them, sent a flood of water streaming down his shirt front. He snatched up the towel and hurled it angrily in the direction of the sink. 'Get that sloppy thing out of here! What kind of game are you playing?'

'I'm not playing any game,' Karen said unsteadily. 'You shouldn't have grabbed me like that.'

'I thought you'd be happy to see me.'

'I was,' Karen said. 'I mean, I *am*.'

'You've got a funny way of showing it. "Not here, Tim, please," like I'm asking you to do something criminal.'

'I didn't mean it like that,' Karen said. 'Can't it wait till tonight? We do have a date, don't we?'

'I don't know. Do we? Maybe you'd rather go out with somebody who turns you on more.'

'Tim, don't be this way.'

'How do you expect me to be? A guy tries to kiss his girl, and she acts like he's some sort of sex fiend. What's he supposed to do, feel flattered?'

Karen turned back to the baby.

'I'm sorry, but I can't help it. It's the Zenners' house. I shouldn't even have let you in.'

'You don't need to worry; I'm headed straight back out again. I'll leave you to your peace and purity. Have a blast with your little angels.'

'Thanks. I intend to.'

Biting down on her lower lip to keep it from trembling, Karen busied herself unstrapping the baby. She clung to her self-control until she heard the front door slam, and then, as she had been afraid would happen, her eyes filled with tears. She swiped at them angrily with the back of her hand. How could she let herself get this upset over such a silly argument? She had been in the right. She knew that, and Tim must also. When you were right about something you should stick by your guns, shouldn't you?

But what if I've lost him? The words sprang into her mind so quickly that it was as though they had been lurking just beneath the edge of her consciousness. *What if he doesn't show up tonight? What if I never go out with him again?*

Which was absurd, of course. All couples had arguments. All you had to do to know that was to turn on television. It was a normal part of dating to have spats and make up after them. The girls in TV dramas even seemed to enjoy it.

But those girls were most of them so glib and self-confident that they never worried about anything. They shuffled their stacks of lovers as though they were playing cards, secure in the fact that if they lost one hand they would be dealt another. They didn't have the slightest idea what it was like to be a high school senior and never in your life have had anyone in love with you.

'It's unnatural,' Karen's mother had observed accusingly. 'When I was your age, I was out at parties every weekend.'

'People don't have "parties" these days,' Karen had told her. 'They have "get-togethers".'

'Don't be smart with me. Whatever they are, you ought to be part of them. There's no reason for you to be spending so much time by yourself. If you'd just make a little effort to socialise—'

'I don't want to socialise.'

That had been a lie. She had not realised how much of one, however, until that day in the cafeteria when Tim Dietz had stood in line behind her and made a joking remark about the amount of ketchup she was taking for her hamburger. As they left the counter, he had fallen into step beside her and said, 'Look – we're in luck! There're some empty seats over there.'

They had eaten together, and he had asked her about an upcoming English test. Which poems were they to study?

Did she understand them? How many stanzas were they supposed to memorise? He had commented on her sweater: 'Brown-eyed blondes look good in green.'

When the bell rang to signal the end of lunch period, he had asked her if she had plans for that coming Friday.

'I'll call you. Maybe we can take in a show or something.'

She had not believed him. That evening he had called, and she still had not believed it, had not been able to imagine herself on Friday, answering the doorbell to find Tim standing there, or sitting in a movie theatre next to him or walking beside him into Hamburger Haven.

But it had happened. The miracle had occurred, and as though some fairy godmother had waved the wand, she had been transformed overnight it seemed from a nonentity into a real person. The strange years lay behind her, that odd, directionless time of drifting and dreaming. She now had an identity; she was 'Karen Connors, Tim Dietz's girl-friend', the attractive blonde who wore green sweaters.

What if I've lost him!

But she hadn't, she told herself firmly, fighting down the panic. Couples didn't break up over a few cross words and a wet dish towel. They did have a date tonight. Tim wouldn't break it. Oh, he would undoubtedly start off acting stiff and cool, but by the end of the evening they would be parked somewhere, probably up on the hill, and everything would be all right again. It *would* be that way. It *had* to be.

Stephanie was becoming restless. She gave a demanding grunt and held up her arms to be lifted.

'Sleepytime?' Karen suggested as she gathered her up.

When she realised where it was they were headed, Stephanie let out a howl of protest and began to struggle. A short time later, however, freshly diapered and tucked into her crib, she had settled into placid acceptance of the inevitable. With a thumb in her mouth and the other hand methodically twisting a lock of fine brown hair, she gazed up at Karen with heavy-lidded eyes.

'Sleep tight,' Karen said, bending to kiss her. The cheek beneath her lips was as smooth and soft as a flower petal. 'You're beautiful,' she whispered to the drowsy baby. 'When you're grown up, all the boys will be fighting over you.'

Leaving the bedroom door propped open a few inches, Karen returned to the kitchen. She picked up the overturned Jell-O bowl and rewet the dish towel to wipe down the high chair. Kids could be exhausting, she conceded to herself. There were girls at school who were adamant about their intention of choosing careers and 'freedom' in place of motherhood.

For herself, Karen could not imagine a life without children. The restrictions imposed by parenthood would be nothing, she was certain, compared with the joys of mothering a child like Stephanie. Or Bobby. Exasperated as she got with him, she had to admit that he was lovable. With his dark wavy hair, he would probably grow up to look something like Tim. If she and Tim were to one day marry, their own child might—

She broke off that train of thought abruptly, it was such a ridiculous thing to be contemplating. Just because they were dating didn't mean their relationship would be permanent. There were dozens of girls who would give their eyeteeth to go out with Tim Dietz. After that scene today, he was probably already having second thoughts about tying himself down to somebody like Karen.

What if I've lost him!

With a major effort of will, Karen set her mind on preparing lunch for herself and Bobby. She located the bread. The jam. The peanut butter. Was there fruit in the refrigerator? Yes, oranges and apples. Which did Bobby like better? Well, that didn't matter; she'd set out both. She poured the milk into two glasses, one for each of them.

Cookies? She checked the ceramic jar on the counter. It was well stocked, as always.

It was seldom that the Zenners took a day to themselves without the children. Today they had gone to the horse races in Santa Fe.

'Some friends are celebrating their anniversary,' Mrs Zenner had explained to Karen, almost apologetically. 'They want us to spend the day with them. I told them we wouldn't consider it unless we could get you to babysit. There's nobody else I'd trust the kids with for that long.'

'I have a date that night,' Karen had told her, 'but I can sit until six or so if that's all you need. Don't worry about anything. The kids and I always get along fine.'

The table was ready. She put the cookies on a plate and went into the living room to call Bobby in from the front yard. When she opened the door, the brilliant beauty of a New Mexico spring burst full upon her, crisp and sparkling and radiant. The rains that had fallen so heavily during the early part of the week had left the air fragrant and fresh. The poplars that lined the yard glistened pale green against the rich blue of the sky, and a slight breeze rustled through them, making them shimmer like aspen. The lawn still held the brown of winter, but daffodils and crocuses were like bright flags, bordering the slate rock path that led from the driveway to the house.

Yes, the day was beautiful. But where were the children?

Karen scanned the empty yard in bewilderment. 'Bobby!'

She awaited a response, a burst of giggles from behind the snowball bushes at the side of the house or a shout from a neighbouring yard. The silence that she had been longing for earlier lay heavy about her.

'Bobby!' she called again and then again with increasing impatience.

Eventually, when it became apparent that there was to be no answer, she turned and re-entered the house.

2

Karen's immediate reaction to Bobby's disappearance was less one of worry than of exasperation. The Zenners lived in a pleasant suburban neighbourhood where dangers were few. The people who occupied the attractive brick homes along the tree-lined streets all knew each other, and children wandered from house to house, shifting location when boredom set in or cookie supplies ran low.

The youngsters who had been there that morning had not been invited over; they had simply arrived. Any reservations Karen might have had about asking them in had been overcome by the enthusiasm of Bobby's greeting – 'Hey, Pete! Hi, Kevin!' – and the momentum with which the three of them had gone bounding past her in to Bobby's bedroom. Now, just as naturally, they must have moved on to some other play area. What was annoying was that, despite his promise not to leave the yard, Bobby had gone with them.

Well, she would just have to find him and haul him back, Karen told herself. He had undoubtedly gone to the home of one of the other children. This knowledge, while reassuring, was not particularly helpful. Although they had looked familiar, especially the freckled boy with the red hair, and she was sure they had been over on other occasions, she had no idea where either of them lived.

On the back of the kitchen phone directory, Mrs Zenner had listed emergency numbers for the police, the fire department, and the family doctor. There was also a list of numbers of personal friends. Karen scanned these quickly. Most of the names came in pairs and were evidently those of couples, but towards the bottom of the page there were some boys' names listed singly. Although there was no 'Kevin', she did find a 'Peter Johnson'.

Dialling the number opposite it, Karen listened impatiently to the repeated sound of the ringing telephone. Just as she was ready to hang up, there was a click and the sudden background sound of a crying baby.

After a brief pause, a woman's voice said, 'Hello?'

'Is this Mrs Johnson?' Karen asked. 'Peter Johnson's mother?'

'Yes, it is.' The woman sounded harried. 'Pete's not here right now.'

'I'm Karen Connors,' Karen told her. 'I'm the Zenners' babysitter, and I'm trying to track down Bobby. I was hoping he might be at your place.'

'Nobody's here,' said Mrs Johnson. 'I thought Pete was going over to Bobby's. That's what he said when he ran out of here this morning.'

'He was here earlier,' said Karen. 'Then they both took off some place. There was another boy with them. I think Bobby called him "Kevin".'

'That would have been Kevin Springer,' said Mrs Johnson. 'They've probably gone to his house. You can't call there; they have an unlisted number. It's the big, two-storey house on the corner of Elm and Hawthorne, if you want to go over there.'

'I guess I'll have to if Bobby doesn't show up soon.' Karen was growing increasingly irritated as the conversation continued. 'Do they always do things like this? Just go running off, I mean?'

'Let's just say it isn't the first time,' said Mrs Johnson. 'If you do go over there, you tell Peter—'

There was a pause. Against the thin, hornet's wail of the baby, Karen could hear the muffled thud of a slamming door.

'Is that you, Pete?' Mrs Johnson's voice rose sharply, channelled away from the telephone. There was a mumbled response; then Peter's mother was back again. 'It's him, all right. At least he's got enough sense to know when he's hungry.'

I wish Bobby did, Karen thought ruefully as she replaced the receiver on the hook.

The Zenners' home was on Elm Street. The 'corner of Elm and Hawthorne' was half a block away. Should she try to go there now? Karen wondered. Stephanie was sleeping soundly, and the round trip to the Springers' should take no more than ten minutes. At the same time, she didn't like the idea of leaving the child alone in the house, even for that short a period. Freak accidents did occur; you read about them in the paper. Fires broke out, or babies twisted in their sleep and got caught between the slats of their cribs.

If Bobby was old enough to wander, he was old enough to come home. It wasn't as though there were anything to really worry over. Mrs Johnson's calm reaction had made it obvious that this disappearing act was nothing unusual for neighbourhood youngsters.

Karen set the second milk glass back in the refrigerator and sat down at the kitchen table to eat her own lunch. After the noise and activity of the morning, the house seemed strangely silent. With nothing to distract her, it was difficult to keep her mind from returning to the argument with Tim. If they *did* break up—

We won't! We can't!

But if they *did*—

Would I go back, Karen asked herself, to what I was before?

When it came to that, what *had* she been before that had been so markedly different from what she was now? It was not as though there had been a physical transformation. The pale hair and brown eyes that people now seemed to find attractive were the same hair and eyes that she had had the semester before. The slender, small-boned body which Tim thought 'sexy' had developed at approximately the same time as the bodies of other girls.

So what had caused the strangeness? Even her own mother had felt it. 'Karen is not quite like other children.' How many times had Mrs Connors repeated that statement – to relatives – to teachers – to mothers of grammar school classmates who expressed concern because 'that sweet little girl seems to be alone so much'?

'Karen is different,' her mother would tell them, laughing a little as though to soften the starkness of the revelation. 'She's a very distinct individual, our daughter Karen.'

Why had she been different? She hadn't chosen to be. She had, in fact, gone out of her way to conform. She had worn jeans when the other girls wore jeans; she had worn dresses when they wore dresses. During those years when straight hair was the 'in' thing, she had grown hers long and let it swing loose and shiny over her shoulders. During 'curly' years, she had worn it short and set it nightly in pincurls. She had performed well in school, but not so well that she stood out from the others. She could not have been branded a 'grind', any more than she could have been labelled 'stupid'. She was average. Just like everybody. Except—

Except that she *wasn't*.

The difference could not be seen, but it had existed for as long as she could remember, separating her from her classmates like an invisible wall. It wasn't that they disliked her; they were simply not quite comfortable around her, and when they formed their groups she did not have a place in them. During her early years she had been hurt by this. Eventually, she had managed to convince herself that it didn't matter. She had her reading, her babysitting, her summer job at the Day Care Centre. She did not need teenage companions. There was nothing they could provide for her that she could not equally well provide for herself.

Or so she had rationalised. It had not been true.

We're not breaking up. It was just a little argument.

I won't think about it, Karen told herself firmly. There are other things to think about.

For instance, Bobby. Something had to be done about locating Bobby. It was now one-thirty, a full hour past his usual lunchtime.

Shoving back her chair, Karen got up from the table and went to look in on Stephanie. The baby was sleeping heavily. Her thumb had slipped from her mouth, and the small, soft hand was curled against her cheek like an unopened flower. Her chest rose and fell with her slow, steady breathing.

'I'm sorry, sweetie,' Karen said softly. 'I know it's not fair to disturb you, but I don't know what else to do.'

Bending over the crib, she made an awkward attempt to gather the child up into her arms. Stephanie whimpered and bunched herself together, refusing to open her eyes. When Karen finally had her hoisted against her shoulder, she sagged there, limp as a sack of potatoes, making small pathetic snuffles of protest.

'I guess you'll have to make the trip by stroller,' Karen said with a sigh.

For that to be accomplished, she had to return Stephanie to the crib while she went in search of the stroller and got it unfolded. Then she got the baby up again and put shoes on her feet and worked her arms into the sleeves of a sweater. By the time she had completed preparations, another twenty minutes had elapsed and it was practically two o'clock.

There's no excuse for this, Karen fumed silently as she hurried along, trying to keep from jolting the nodding baby. Bobby knows better than to run off this way.

It was obvious immediately that the brick house on the corner was one in which neighbourhood youngsters habitually congregated. An assortment of bats and balls and other play equipment littered the front lawn, and a bevy of bicycles crowded the driveway. A blue windbreaker – Bobby's? – was draped across a bush, and three pairs of roller skates were piled in a heap on the front doorstep.

The moment she rang the bell, Karen could hear pounding feet stampeding from several directions, and when the door was thrown open she found herself confronted by two small blonde girls and a redhaired boy whom she recognised as one of the two youngsters who had been over that morning.

'I'm here to get Bobby,' she told them.

The girls stared at her blankly.

The boy said, 'Bob's not here.'

'Where is he, then?' Karen asked impatiently. She could imagine Bobby crouched, giggling, just out of sight behind the door.

The boy shrugged. 'I guess he's back at his house.'

'If he were,' Karen said, 'I wouldn't have had to come over here to find him. Is your mother home?'

'Yeah. You want me to get her?'

At Karen's curt nod, all three children disappeared from the doorway. The boy reappeared a few moments later, accompanied by a woman with the same rust-coloured hair as his own.

'Kev says you're looking for the Zenner boy,' she said. 'I haven't seen him at all today.'

'Are you sure?' Karen pressed her. 'Mrs Johnson seemed to think that all the boys were playing over here.'

'Pete was, for a while, but I don't think Bobby was.' Mrs Springer turned to Kevin. 'Was he over here, Kev? Don't play games, now. I'm going to be real upset if you know where he is and you're not telling.'

Kevin shook his head. 'We wanted him to come, but we couldn't find him.'

'Couldn't find him!' exclaimed Karen. 'What do you mean?'

'We were playing hide-and-seek,' Kevin told her. 'I found Pete right off, but Bobby hid real good.'

'And you left? You just left, without finishing the game?'

'I called "All-y – all-y – in – free!" ' Kevin said defensively. 'He could've come home free if he'd wanted to.'

'But that was hours ago!' Karen protested. 'If Bobby was hiding in his yard, he would have seen you leave. There wouldn't have been any reason for him to have stayed hidden after that.'

'I wouldn't worry,' Mrs Springer said. 'You know how boys are with sitters – they love to give them a hard time. When you get back to the house, you'll more than likely find him waiting.'

'No, I won't,' Karen said with certainty. 'Bobby isn't at his house. He isn't anywhere around there.'

'Now, how can you know that?' Mrs Springer asked reasonably.

'I just do,' Karen told her.

There was no explanation to offer. She did not try to find one. She had learned to accept without question knowledge that came to her in this abrupt and chilling manner, because experience had taught her that it was always right.

3

'Seven years old, brown hair, brown eyes, wearing jeans and a yellow T-shirt.'

The sandy-haired policeman with the vivid blue eyes, who had introduced himself on his arrival as 'Officer Ronald Wilson', read back the description Karen had given him. He was young – much too young, in Karen's opinion, to have been sent to handle something as important as a missing-child report.

'Is there anything you want to add to that?' he asked her, his eyes on his notes. 'What about his shoes – were they leather, or was he wearing sneakers? How about outer clothing? Did he have on a sweater or jacket?'

'I think he was wearing tennis shoes,' said Karen. 'The jacket was a windbreaker – blue, maybe, or green. His friends might remember. Kevin Springer and Peter Johnson were with him this morning.'

Officer Wilson jotted down the names 'Springer' and 'Johnson' beneath Bobby's physical description. Watching his hands as he wrote, Karen couldn't help noticing that his fingernails were bitten down to the quick. The discovery did little to enhance his image as an authority figure.

'The Springers live just down the street on the corner,' she told him. 'I don't have an address for the Johnsons, but I can get you the phone number.'

'I'll call them from here, then.' He retracted the point of his ballpoint with a quick snap. 'I wouldn't start worrying yet, if I were you. Kids like to wander. We get a half-dozen calls like this one every week, and most of the time the kids turn up on their own.'

'And the rest of the time?'

'We find them someplace. Usually it's at a video game

hall. Or a Radio Shack. There's something about those Radio Shacks that draws them like flies.'

'He hasn't gone to Radio Shack.'

There was no way that she could imagine Bobby's having taken off on his own for the places mentioned. If he had been with other boys, it might have been plausible, but he would not have gone by himself. Besides, to her knowledge there were no game rooms or electronics stores within walking distance.

'He hasn't just wandered,' Karen said. 'He's trapped somewhere.'

'He's *trapped*?'

'He isn't able to come home. He wants to, but he can't.' She was making no sense, not even to herself. 'I don't know why I think that, but I do.'

'That's not very likely,' said Officer Wilson. 'Despite what you'd think from watching those police shows on television, kidnappings don't occur often. When a kid this age disappears, he's usually run off to a friend's house. Have you been able to get hold of the parents?'

'No,' Karen said. 'They're at the races in Santa Fe. There's no way to reach them.'

'If Bobby hasn't turned up by the time they get home, have them call the station,' Officer Wilson told her. 'My guess, though, is that he'll be back before they are.'

He made a quick call to the Johnsons' from the telephone in the kitchen. Then he left, saying that he would stop at both the Johnsons' house and the Springers' on his way back to the police station.

When the door closed behind him, Stephanie, who had been confined to her playpen during the interview, began to fuss for attention. Karen hoisted her up over the railing and took her out to the kitchen. She strapped her into her high chair and poured orange juice into a plastic cup that was decorated with a picture of Kermit the Frog.

'Here – drink your froggie juice,' Karen said softly to the baby.

The kitchen seemed unnaturally quiet. In the dreamlike silence, she could hear the tick of the clock on the far wall and the sound of Stephanie swallowing and the steady, rhythmic beating of her own heart. The late afternoon sunlight slanted in through the window over the sink and painted one side of the room with great splashes of gold. Dust motes swirled and drifted in rainbow clusters, reflecting the light like prisms. Beyond the glass the poplars shimmered and shivered with a silvery radiance.

Karen leaned against the counter and closed her eyes.

Bobby's caught in a box. Incredibly, she could actually see him there, curled quiet in darkness. He had been frightened, terribly frightened; the intensity of his terror had left a lingering residue like the stale odour of cigarette smoke in an empty room. The smell of fear was mixed with other scents – sweat and grease and urine. Bobby's eyes were closed, and his hair lay damp and matted upon his forehead. His knees were drawn tight against his chest.

She had been right about the windbreaker. It was blue.

'Dear God,' Karen whispered, 'please, let him be alive!'

A boy in a *box*, not a video hall or theatre! The police would not find him there; they would not be looking for boxes. 'Bobby's closed in a box' – the statement was ridiculous. She could shriek it to the skies, and there would be no way in the world that any sane person would ever believe her.

The frog cup clanked hard upon the metal tray of the high chair.

'Cookie!' Stephanie announced loudly. 'Cookie – me!'

Karen's eyes flew open, and the vision snapped out of existence. She was back in the Zenners' kitchen, and she had been dreaming. Dreaming or hallucinating. How long had she been standing there, propped against the counter like a zombie? Five minutes? Ten? The baby's cup was empty. The light from the window had subtly shifted. The sun had slipped behind the poplars, and its softened rays were filtered by the branches. The floor of the kitchen was dappled with shadows.

'Cookie!' Stephanie demanded impatiently.

'Yes, sweetie – cookie.'

The cookies were still on the table where she had set them at lunchtime. Karen got one for Stephanie, loosened the safety strap, and lifted her down from the chair. The kitchen clock read five past five. The Zenners would be returning at any time now. What would she tell them – 'Stephanie's here, but I've misplaced Bobby'? With all the articles of advice offered in teen publications, she could never remember seeing one on the subject of how to break the news to parents that one of their children was missing.

He's in a box. The words came whispering back to her. If she closed her eyes again she knew that she would be sucked back into it, that waking dream of heavy, oily darkness.

What sort of box and where could he have found it? Her mind leapt spasmodically from one supposition to another. An empty packing crate? An abandoned refrigerator? Those were junkyard items, not likely to be found in a residential neighbourhood. According to Kevin, the game of hide-and-seek had been played in the Zenners' own yard. Why, then, did she feel this overpowering certainty that Bobby was not in the vicinity?

'Cookie – me?' The chirp of a hopeful voice brought her out of her reverie. A small, sticky hand was tugging imploringly at her jeans.

'You just had one,' Karen responded automatically. 'You'll spoil your supper.'

'Me? Cookie – me?'

What did it matter? There would be no family dinner that evening anyway. Karen placed the plate where Stephanie could reach it and seated herself in a chair across from her. She watched the child as she ate and tried not to let herself think about anything except the demise of the cookies and what a mess a toddler could make with them, while beyond the kitchen window the world mellowed into twilight and the sky changed from blue to lavender behind the darkening shapes of the trees.

At five forty-seven the Zenners got back from Santa Fe. By five fifty Mrs Zenner was weeping hysterically and her husband was engaged in making the first of many frantic phone calls. The police were resummoned, and on this return trip the young blue-eyed officer appeared to be taking the situation seriously. Mrs Johnson came over, bringing her son Peter and Kevin Springer. No new information surfaced. The boys' stories were compatible. They had been playing, and Bobby had hidden. It was the last they had seen of him. When he had refused to respond to Kevin's summons to come 'home free', they had gone off to play at the Springers'.

In the midst of the interrogation, the telephone rang. The call was for Karen, and she took it on the kitchen extension. The voice that greeted her was her mother's, pitched, as usual, into a tone of accusation.

'What's going on over there? Wasn't that Mrs Zenner who answered the phone? If they've got back, why aren't you home yet?'

'Bobby's missing,' Karen told her.

'What do you mean, *missing*?'

'He went out to play around noon and didn't come back.'

'It's after seven!' exclaimed Mrs Connors.

'Don't you think I know that? The police are here. Everybody's worried sick.'

'I should think they would be!'

'I feel terrible,' Karen said. 'I should have kept better watch over him.'

'They can't hold you responsible,' her mother said.

26

'You're a conscientious sitter. If that boy went running off someplace—'

'That's not what happened.'

'Then, what *did* happen? Children don't just vanish. You've told me yourself that Bobby runs you to death when you babysit.'

He's in a box. There was no way she could say it – not to the police – not to the Zenners – not to her mother. She was beginning to wonder if she was going crazy. How could she be so certain of something that was impossible?

'You'd better come home,' Mrs Connors said. 'Unless there's something specific they need you for, you're undoubtedly more in the way over there than anything else.'

'I can't just walk out!' Karen objected. 'Mom, this is serious!'

'Tim's here,' her mother told her. 'He says you have a date.'

'That's right, we did.' Unbelievable as such a thing would have seemed earlier, she had forgotten about that completely. 'Tell him what's happened, will you, Mom? Tell him I'm sorry.'

'Why don't I send him over to pick you up?'

'I told you,' Karen said, 'I can't just leave like that.'

'What are you planning to do, spend the night there?'

'I don't know,' Karen told her helplessly. 'I don't know what I ought to do. Maybe someone will need me for something.'

'Get your things together,' her mother said firmly. 'I'm sending Tim to get you. I've a splitting headache, Karen, and I don't want to argue.'

'Mom, I can't. I'm the one – the only one who *knows*!'

About the box! The unspoken statement surged back into her consciousness, urgent, discordant. No longer were the words mere whispers, hissing bewildering warnings. Now they were louder, stronger, rushing into her head with a thunderous roar.

'I can't come home,' Karen repeated shakily. 'Not until we learn what's happened.'

Without waiting for a response, she placed the phone back on the hook and raised her hands to her head. Her heart was pounding so hard that when she pressed her fingertips against her temples she could feel the pulsation of blood. The vision was back, more vivid than before, projected like a movie upon the screen of her brain. Although Bobby was encased in darkness, she could see him as clearly as though it were daylight. He had not changed position, but he seemed to have slid forward so that one side of his face was resting against metal.

For a long time Karen stood with her eyes closed, focusing with another, inner, eye upon the inert figure. Then, just as she was beginning to feel that she had absorbed every detail, something began to happen. Although Bobby was lying so still that it was impossible to tell whether or not he was breathing, she was aware of the sensation of motion, as though he were in some mysterious manner moving towards her.

I *am* crazy, Karen told herself with numb acceptance. The hidden strangeness had finally surfaced, as she had always feared in some dark recess of her mind that it someday would. In the space of one afternoon she had managed to lose all control of her senses. *Bobby is moving, and yet he isn't!* Her head was spinning, and the pressure was mounting so rapidly that she was afraid that her skull might burst. With her eyes still shut, she pressed her cheek against the cool, rough surface of the kitchen wall, struggling desperately to regain a grip on reality.

She could smell urine. In his initial moment of terror, Bobby had soiled himself. She could smell perspiration and grease of a kind she associated with the lubrication of mechanical objects. There was another odour also, one that she had not formerly been aware of – the faint, sickening emanation of automobile exhaust.

Exhaust fumes! Bobby's box is in a car! Karen caught her breath as the realisation swept over her. He was in a car, and that car had gone into motion! He was with somebody who was taking him someplace – but *where*?

She released her hold on the image, and her eyes flew open. She was back in the Zenners' kitchen, and she was trembling.

'Karen?' Mr Zenner spoke from the doorway. 'You're not still on the phone, are you? The police officer doesn't want us to tie up the line. He wants it kept open in case Bobby tries to reach us.'

'I'm not on it,' Karen said. 'I only talked for a minute.'

She moved away from the wall. Her cheek was raw from the pressure of the plaster.

'Mr Zenner,' she said hesitantly, 'I have this feeling about Bobby. I think he's in a car.'

'What makes you say that?' Bobby's father asked sharply. 'Do you know something more than you've told us? Did Bobby go off with someone?'

'I don't know anything for sure,' Karen said. 'It's just a feeling.'

'Then keep it to yourself,' Mr Zenner told her. 'We've got enough on our minds without having to listen to premonitions. If you'd done your job, our boy would be here now.'

He's in a car, and it's coming closer! She wanted to grab him to shake him, to force the words upon him, but there was no way that she could do so. Why should he believe her? Why should *anyone*?

Mr Zenner went back to the living room, and Karen followed. There were more people there now than there had been when she had left. A dark-haired woman whose resemblance to Mrs Zenner was so marked that she had to be a relative was seated beside her on the sofa, weeping softly and clutching a squirming Stephanie. Kevin's parents had arrived along with their two daughters.

The young police officer, looking uncomfortably out of control of things, was standing in the archway between the living room and dining area.

Karen went over to him. She knew it would do no good, but she had to tell him.

'Bobby Zenner is in a car,' she said quietly.

He stared at her. 'What are you talking about?'

'He's in a car,' Karen repeated. 'I don't know how I know it, but I do. I don't expect you to believe me.'

The doorbell chimed.

'What kind of car?' Officer Wilson asked her.

'A Pontiac.' The words left her lips before she realised that she was going to speak them, and they took her by surprise.

'Is it a car you've seen before?' He was regarding her intently. His eyes were the strangest shade of blue she had ever seen, and they were riveted on her face.

'Yes. Yes – I think—'

She didn't 'think' – she *knew*! It was a green Pontiac with a dent in the right front fender. There was a bumper sticker on the back that read 'Have You Hugged A Jock Today?' The vinyl on the front seat had a rip in it, and a spring stuck a little way through so that when you sat down you had to be careful that it didn't snag your clothes.

The chimes sounded again. Mr Zenner went to the door and opened it.

'Yes?' he asked curtly.

'I'm here to pick up Karen,' said the person who stood outside on the darkened doorstep. 'Her folks sent me over for her.'

Karen glanced up quickly at the familiar voice. In one blinding flash, the answer was upon her. The pieces of the puzzle fell into place.

'Yes, I do know the car,' she said softly. 'The boy who owns it is right there.'

4

When Karen arrived home her parents were watching television. She was greeted in the front entrance hall by the sound of canned laughter rolling out from the den in a senseless roar. The stairway beckoned, and she was tempted to bolt straight up it and run to her room. Then she sighed, accepted the inevitable, and, bracing herself for the tirade of questions that she knew awaited her, went down the hall to the wood-panelled den.

They were seated, as she had known they would be, in recliners opposite the television set. The angle of the light from the lamp on the table between them accentuated the difference in their ages, glinting off of the youthful highlights in her mother's blonde hair and turning her father's to silver.

'They found Bobby,' Karen announced. 'He's OK.'

'Thank God!' said her father, reaching over to adjust the volume of the television so they could hear each other. 'Where was he?'

'In the trunk of Tim's car.'

'He was where?' exclaimed Mrs Connors.

'He was shut in Tim's car trunk,' Karen repeated. 'Tim changed a tyre this morning, and when he put back the jack, he didn't slam the door down hard enough. Bobby was playing hide-and-seek and climbed into the trunk to hide.'

'Do you mean Tim was with you at the Zenners'?' her mother asked her.

'Just for a couple of minutes,' said Karen. 'When he started to leave, he noticed the trunk was gaping open, so he slammed it. Of course, he didn't know anyone was in there, and Bobby was too startled to yell.'

'It's a wonder the boy didn't suffocate,' her father said.

'It was close. He was unconsc

'Tim never should have been ι

'You know you're not allowed to have aid her mother sitting. How did you get home?' rs when you're

'Tim brought me.'

'They didn't hold him for questioning?'

'No,' Karen said. 'It wasn't as though he anything deliberate.'

'Well, I hope you've learned from this experien,' said Mrs Connors. 'It could easily have ended in tragedy.'

'I know that, Mom.'

'You'll never be offered another job at the Zenners'. They'll tell other people, too. This is the sort of thing that gets around.'

'Yes, I know.'

'There's no sense in beating a dead horse, Wanda,' Mr Connors interjected. 'Karen's learned a lesson, and, as it turns out, there's a happy ending.'

He reached again for the knob on the television set. The volume came surging up, and sounds of hysterical gaiety filled the room.

Karen regarded her father with gratitude. For once his detached approach to life seemed less a fault than a virtue. 'I'm tired,' she said against the noise. 'I'm going up to bed.'

She climbed the stairs to the second floor and went down the hall to her room. The door stood ajar, and she pushed it open and turned on the light. Pale blue curtains billowed gently at either side of the open window, and the lavender flowered spread that covered the bed gave the impression of a garden filled with forget-me-nots. A white porcelain lamp stood on the bedside table, and a shelf that ran the length of the wall held a collection of costumed dolls left over from Karen's childhood.

This room was the one space in the house that was completely her own. The watercolour landscapes that brightened the walls were pictures she herself had selected.

...ed with volumes of her own choosing,
The bookcase ...vels and romances, not the news publi-
poetry, histo... kept piled on the living-room coffee table
cations her ...f-the-Month-Club selections her mother
or the B...
subscrib...
Closi... ...e door, Karen stood quiet for a moment, letting
the roo... ...s peace become a part of her. Then she drew a
deep ...ath and crossed the room to the window. The cool
night air, faintly perfumed with the scent of hyacinths,
brush... against her face, and night noises rose lightly to
her ears. She could hear the soft rustle of new leaves whispering as a breeze stirred through them. A dog barked once
in a neighbouring yard, and there was the sound of a door
being opened and slammed shut.

Somewhere a baby cried. The thin, far wail came muffled
by distance, like an echo from a dream. She listened as it
rose and fell and rose again and then died away into silence.

She could not remember ever having been this tired.

She turned from the window, flicked off the light switch,
and moved through the darkness to the bed. Sinking down
upon it, she was immediately overcome by exhaustion. Her
arms and legs settled into the mattress like leaden weights.
The moment her head touched the pillow, sleep descended
like a heavy blanket, closing out the world.

In hours or perhaps only minutes – there was no way of
guessing which – Karen was jarred awake by a sharp, stac-
cato rapping. She tried to shove the sound away, but even
as she did so she knew that it would continue until she
responded. She felt no surprise. Somewhere, deep inside
her, she had realised all along that it was not going to be
this easy. The day's events were bound to cause some
repercussion beyond the mild question-and-answer
sequence in the den.

'Karen?' It was her mother's voice.

'Yes,' Karen mumbled.

'You're not asleep yet, are you? May I come in?'

'Sure, if you want to.' Why had she bothered asking? She would have come in anyway, regardless of the answer.

Karen heard the sound of the knob turning and forced her eyes open in response to the sudden splash of light from the hall.

Her mother stood silhouetted in the doorway.

'You never said how they found him,' she said.

'He was in the trunk of Tim's car,' Karen said groggily.

'That's *where* they found him, not *how*. Why did they look there? How did they get the idea of opening the trunk?'

'I told them to,' said Karen.

'And what gave *you* that idea?'

'It was a guess.'

'That makes no sense,' said Mrs Connors. 'People don't guess things like that. You have to have had some reason for thinking Bobby would be in there.' She entered the room and came over to stand next to the bed. 'I want you to tell me how it happened. I want you to tell me exactly how you knew Bobby was in that trunk.'

'There's nothing to tell,' Karen insisted. 'I had a feeling, that's all. I told the policeman, and he had Tim open the trunk, and Bobby was there. Why does it matter so much? Bobby's been found, hasn't he? Isn't that what's important?'

'Of course, that's important,' Mrs Connors conceded. 'It's also important that you get this story into some sort of order. When Tim left the Zenners' this morning, you probably saw him out. When you turned to go back inside, you could have heard the trunk lid slam. The sound registered in your subconscious, and later, when Tim arrived at the door, you suddenly remembered it.'

'That's not what happened,' Karen protested. 'When Tim left, I was back in the kitchen with Stephanie.'

Mrs Connors was silent. For a moment, Karen allowed herself to hope that the conversation had been completed.

What more, she wondered, could her mother find to ask her?

The question, when it did come, was completely out of context.

'Do you remember Mickey Duggin?'

'Who?' Karen said blankly.

'The Duggins lived next door to us when we were in that duplex over on Fourth Street.'

'That was for ever ago!' Karen regarded her mother in bewilderment. 'How could I remember something that far back? We moved here the year I started first grade.'

'You were five at the time I'm talking about. Mickey was three. We shared a backyard with the Duggins, except you stayed in it and Mickey didn't. His mother was always standing at the side of the house and yelling for him, and you'd stand there, just inside the gate, and cry your eyes out because you were afraid he was lost. Then she'd find him and bring him home and spank him, and you'd cry some more because you didn't want him punished. Don't you remember that?'

'No,' Karen said.

'Well, anyway, there was one day when Mickey took off the way he always did, but this time they couldn't find him. Mrs Duggin called her husband home from work, and by the end of the afternoon they had the whole neighbourhood out looking. The child wasn't anywhere. And he was so little, hardly more than a baby. There just wasn't anywhere for him to *go*.'

'Did they call the police?' Karen asked, interested despite herself.

'Of course, but that didn't do any good. They didn't know where to look any more than the parents did. You were terribly upset. I tried to keep you inside, away from things, but with all the commotion and people coming and going next door, you had to know what was happening. Your father was working late that night and didn't come home for dinner. You wouldn't touch the supper I fixed you, and I heard you crying after I'd put you to bed. Then you settled down, and I thought you were asleep. Maybe you were. Maybe you dreamed it.'

Karen was totally caught up now. 'Dreamed what? What are you talking about?'

'It was about nine – maybe nine-thirty – and suddenly you were standing in the door to the living room. I can see it still. You were wearing little shortie pyjamas – it was midsummer – and your eyes were big and scared. And you said, "Mickey's down under the driveway." '

'Under the driveway!' Karen echoed.

'I thought you'd been having a nightmare. You kept saying it over and over, "He's under the driveway! Please, go get him!" Finally – I don't know why; it was just something about the way you kept repeating it, as though you were so certain – I went next door and told the Duggins what you'd been saying. There was a drainage ditch that ran along the side of the street with a pipe that went under all the driveways to let the water through. That's where he was. That's where they found Mickey.'

'In the pipe?'

'He must have crawled in to hide from his mother when he heard her calling. Then he couldn't get out. There was rubble blocking the far end, and he didn't know how to inch out backwards.'

'Was he all right?' Karen asked.

'Yes, except for scratches. He was scared, though. I don't imagine they had any more problems with his leaving the yard.'

'What do you mean, you "don't imagine"?' asked Karen. 'Don't you *know*? After all, we were neighbours.'

'I don't know anything,' her mother said. 'The Duggins didn't communicate with us after that. Neither they nor anyone else in the neighbourhood seemed to want to have anything more to do with us. People talk, especially people like Mrs Duggin. It would have been impossible for that woman to have kept her mouth shut about anything.'

'But, what did they hold against us?' Karen asked her. 'The way you tell it, it sounds like I was a child-heroine. Weren't they grateful?'

'Maybe, at first, they were. By the next morning, though, that part was forgotten. What they hung on to was how weird the whole thing was. You hadn't even been there when Mickey ran off. I'd taken you with me to the grocery store. There was no way you could have seen that little boy crawl into the pipe. But you knew he was there.' She paused and then asked slowly, 'How did you know, Karen?'

'I can't answer that,' said Karen. 'I don't even remember its happening.'

'You remember what happened tonight. It was the same thing this time. You knew about Bobby the same way you knew about Mickey.'

'I keep telling you, this thing with Bobby was a guess.'

'Sure, you can say that,' said Mrs Connors. 'Maybe you even believe it. But it can't be true. Every time, it can't be a guess.'

'Every time? It's only happened twice!'

'No, it hasn't,' her mother said. 'There have been other occasions. There have been things like – well, I know one – there was the Rosetti girl's birthday party back when you were in middle school. You didn't want to go because you said this mean girl was going to be there who would tease you about your braces.'

'You made me go anyway. And she *was* there, and I hated the party.'

'That's true,' said her mother. 'But the girl wasn't somebody you'd met before. She was a cousin, visiting from out of town. How could you have known she even existed, much less that she was horrid?'

'I don't remember,' said Karen. 'I must have overheard

it. Maybe someone was talking about her. What are you trying to do, Mom, make me sound like a freak?'

'That's just what I *don't* want you to sound like,' her mother said. 'That's why I'm upset about what happened tonight. If it was bad after Mickey, this could be worse. Whoever was there at the Zenners' is going to talk, and you can be sure the story is going to get better with every telling. That's why it's important for you to have an explanation to offer, something that will sound reasonable and put an end to the gossip.'

'Let people gossip!' Karen countered. 'I couldn't care less. It's not as though I've done something criminal.'

'Well, *I* care,' her mother said. 'And Tim will care. It's taken you long enough to acquire a social life. Do you want to lose it as the result of one evening? You're the one who used the term *freak*. It's a horrible word. I can't believe a young man like Tim would be very enthusiastic about having it used to describe his girlfriend.'

Karen closed her eyes and willed herself to some far place where the sound of her mother's voice could not reach her. The things she was saying were terrible. They were also ridiculous. No one in his right mind would condemn somebody for having hunches.

'Go away,' she whispered. 'Mom, please, go away.'

The silence that followed lasted for such a long time that Karen was actually beginning to wonder if she *had* gone, when her mother spoke again. This time her voice was softer.

'Karen,' Mrs Connors said, 'there is something I want you to think about. You don't have to talk about it, if you don't want to, but you do have to consider it. It got bad – very bad – for our family after the Mickey Duggin thing. There were notes in the mail. There were phone calls. There were odd people turning up on the doorstep, wanting a look at you. It was disturbing enough, even back when you were a five-year-old, so that I swore to myself that I'd not let it happen again.'

'If it was all that bad, you'd think that at least I'd remember it,' Karen said without opening her eyes.

'It was bad enough,' her mother said, 'so that we decided to leave the neighbourhood. That's the point at which we moved here.'

5

Karen dreamed that night, and the dreams were not pleasant. Although she slept the next morning until noon and fell into bed again immediately after dinner, on Monday she was still dragging beneath the weight of exhaustion.

She sat through her first-period history class, struggling to focus her mind on the teacher's lecture, only to find his words sliding away from her like the Jell-O between Stephanie Zenner's chubby fingers. When the bell rang at the end of the period, she was startled to realise that an entire hour had gone by and she had no recollection of what material had been covered.

Tim was waiting in the hall to walk her to English.

'I tried to call you yesterday,' he said as he fell into step beside her. 'Your mom said you were sleeping. Then I tried last night, and your *dad* said you were sleeping. You must really have zonked out.'

'I was so tired I couldn't think straight,' Karen told him. 'I still am, when it comes to that. That thing with Bobby was a nightmare. When you think about what could have happened—'

'But it didn't. The kid's all right, and no one's pressing charges.' Tim took her arm. 'We came out lucky, so let's put it behind us. To change the subject – did Lisa Honeycutt get hold of you?'

'Lisa Honeycutt?' Karen said. 'No. Why?'

'She's chairman of the Prom Committee,' Tim said. 'She asked me in homeroom this morning if I thought you'd like to be on it.'

'She did?' Karen exclaimed. 'That's a surprise. Lisa and I hardly know each other. We had a couple of classes together last year, but I didn't even think she knew my name.'

'Well, you're wrong,' Tim said. 'She does know it, and she knows that you and I go together. She asked me to emcee the Prom Night floor show, and I think she wants you to help decorate.'

'That would be fun,' Karen said.

At another time she would have been thrilled. It was tradition that the Prom Committee was composed of the most popular seniors, and she had never imagined that she would ever be considered one of them. Today, however, it was as difficult to become excited by the idea of decorating the gym as it had been to get a grip on the history lecture. All she wanted was to go back home and sleep.

By lunchtime, Karen was relieved to find the dullness lessening. Like someone recovering from a long and draining illness, she sat with Tim at the Lettermen's Table, nibbling halfheartedly at a sandwich and listening to the conversation going on around them.

Lisa waved from the far side of the crowded cafeteria and worked her way across the room to join them.

'I guess Tim's told you by now that I'd like to have you on my committee,' she said with a smile. 'The Prom theme is "Springtime", and we're going to fix up the gym like a garden. We'll run streamers across the ceiling to look like rainbows. I thought we could cover the bandstand with paper flowers.'

'That sounds great,' Karen told her. 'I'd love to help.'

That evening, when she shared the news with her mother, Mrs Connors was ecstatic.

'The Prom Committee!' she exclaimed. 'Why, that's marvellous! I worked on the Prom when I was in high school, and it was wonderful fun.' She paused, and then, lowering her voice, asked, 'Did you tell Tim what I suggested you tell him?'

'I didn't have to,' Karen said. 'He didn't ask me about it. He wants to forget the whole thing just like I do.'

'I hope it's that easy,' Mrs Connors said doubtfully.

'It will be,' Karen assured her.

Despite the certainty she put into her voice, she thought back upon their disturbing late-night conversation with discomfort. At the time she had wondered if her mother might, for some reason known only to herself, have been inventing the story of 'Mickey Duggin'. The name was not familiar, and Karen had no recollection of the incident her mother had recounted.

That night, however, she had dreamed about a blond boy of preschool age who was dressed in shorts and a red and white T-shirt. He was playing in a sandbox in a fenced yard, and while the sight of the boy struck no response from her, the house behind him did. Somehow, she knew that she herself had once lived in one section of it.

Karen played no active part in the dream, and the child did not seem aware of her presence. For some time he contented himself with running a toy dump truck back and forth through the sand. After a while he appeared to tire of this activity and climbed out of the box and went over to the gate. It was wooden, with the sort of latch that pops open if you give it a shake. Obviously familiar with the procedure, the boy set out to shake it loose. Then, he gave the gate a forceful shove. When it swung open, he walked out of the yard.

She had dreamed this first on the night her mother had told her about Mickey. Then, the following night, she had dreamed it again. It was as though her mind were nagging at her, *Don't you remember?*

'No, I don't,' Karen answered firmly. 'I don't remember a thing.'

On Monday night, she fell asleep with her thoughts determinedly focused on paper flowers and rainbows, and, if she had dreams, she did not recall them in the morning. By Tuesday, the dragging weariness had totally lifted and she was feeling like her old self.

The remainder of the week passed quickly. With only

six weeks left before school let out for the summer, teachers were moving into the home stretch with their class assignments. Term papers were being scheduled and final projects outlined. The Prom Committee held a meeting at Lisa's house on Wednesday, and Karen was placed in charge of decorating the bandstand. Then, on Thursday, the school paper announced nominations for 'Senior Notables'. While she was not at all surprised to find that Tim had been nominated for 'Best Looking', she was stunned to discover that the two of them were on the ballot for 'Cutest Couple'.

'Why not?' Tim asked, amused at her amazement. 'We're a team, aren't we?'

'Yes,' Karen conceded, 'but still—'

It might not have seemed so to Tim, who took such recognition for granted, but to her this was as much of a miracle as having been chosen for the Prom Committee. She was no longer 'that quiet, blonde girl – Karen Something-or-Other'; she was one half of an acknowledged 'cute couple'. For the rest of that day, she floated in a state of euphoria.

On Friday evening, she and Tim doubled with Lisa and her boyfriend, Gary. By the time Karen fell asleep that night, with the remembered pressure of Tim's goodnight kiss still warm upon her lips, the trauma of the previous weekend had been shoved to the back of her mind.

Because of this, it was especially startling on Saturday morning to be awakened by her mother's urgent voice announcing, 'Karen, there's a policeman here to see you.'

'A policeman?' Karen repeated sleepily. 'A policeman – to see *me*? What does he want?'

'I don't know. He won't tell me,' said Mrs Connors. 'Did something happen last night? You and Tim weren't involved in an accident or anything, were you?'

'No,' Karen told her. 'We went bowling and then to Hamburger Haven and then we came home. No accidents – no problems – nothing.'

'Well, you'd better get dressed and come downstairs,' said her mother. 'Your father had an early golf game with a business friend this morning, so, whatever this is, we'll have to deal with it ourselves.'

'You don't think it could be about Bobby, do you?' Karen asked anxiously. 'He was doing fine when I called last Sunday. His mother said he was outside playing.'

'I have no idea what might have happened,' said her mother. 'Hurry up and get some clothes on, and we'll find out.'

The jeans and shirt that she had worn the night before lay tossed across the back of a chair. Karen hastily pulled them on while her mother waited, and the two of them went downstairs together.

The uniformed man who awaited them in the living room was the same young policeman who had been at the Zenners'. Even if she had not recognised him by the sandy hair and well-gnawed fingernails, there was no way that she could ever have forgotten the colour of his eyes.

'Are you here about Bobby?' she asked him. 'He's still all right, isn't he? Has something more happened?'

'No – no, this is about something else entirely.' Officer Wilson looked as out-of-place in her parents' formal living room as he had in the Zenners' more casual one. Without a notebook to hold on to, he didn't quite seem to know what to do with his hands. 'As far as I know, the Zenner kid's fine. His folks would have been back in touch with us if he wasn't.'

'Please, let's all sit down so we can talk more comfortably.' Mrs Connors gestured them towards the sofa and took her own seat in a wing chair across from it.

To Karen, this seating arrangement seemed to place her mother suddenly in a position of regal authority, as though she had ascended a throne, while both her daughter and the police officer sank ineffectually down into sofa cushions.

'What's the reason for this visit, Officer Wilson?' Mrs

Connors asked once they were seated. 'I assume you're not planning to place us under arrest?'

'Nothing like that,' the young policeman assured her hastily. He paused, obviously uncertain about how to proceed. 'I'm sure your daughter has filled you in on what happened last Saturday. You do know, don't you, about how the kid she was babysitting got himself locked in the trunk of a car?'

'Of course,' said Mrs Connors. 'Karen told us all about it. That must have been a terrifying experience for poor little Bobby. It's a relief to know that he's suffered no ill effects from it.'

'He would have, if he'd stayed in that trunk much longer. There was a tear in the fabric lining that let in some air, but it wasn't enough. The boy was unconscious when we found him.' Officer Wilson turned to Karen. 'How did you know he was in there?'

With effort, she avoided glancing at her mother.

'I heard Tim slam the trunk lid. When he appeared at the door like that, I suddenly realised—'

'I don't buy that,' the police officer said quietly. 'That afternoon, you told me, "Bobby's trapped." You said, "He wants to come home, but he can't." You knew it *then*.'

'That was just a guess,' said Karen.

'Do you "guess" like that often?'

'Everybody occasionally makes lucky guesses,' said Mrs Connors. 'There's certainly nothing all that strange about my daughter's having done it once.'

Ignoring the comment, the police officer continued to address himself to Karen.

'I'm not just prying; there's a reason I need to know this. How much control do you have over this guessing? Can you do it whenever you want to?'

'What do you want me to tell you – that I've got magic powers or something?' Karen meant the question to be sarcastic, but it came out sounding defensive. She paused, and then, her curiosity getting the better of her, she asked, 'Why are you interested?'

'There's another kid missing.'

'There's *another*—'

'Carla Sanchez, age eight. She disappeared last week.'

'It's surprising that there's been nothing about it on television,' said Mrs Connors.

'It hasn't had coverage. There was an article in the paper right after it happened, but it didn't make the front page, and the TV networks didn't pick up on it. The story doesn't have news value because it looks like a custodial kidnapping. The parents are divorced. The dad was in town, and, when he left, he apparently took Carla with him.'

'If the mother has custody, you'd think she could get her back,' said Karen. 'Couldn't she take it to court or something?'

'She could if she knew where to find them. Sanchez is a drifter. He's never held a job for more than a few months at a time. It's hard to trace somebody like that. The mother dotes on that little girl. She's going up the walls.'

'That's sad,' Karen said. 'I'm sorry.'

'Yeah, it's sad.' Officer Wilson was silent a moment. Then he said, 'I was hoping that, maybe, you'd want to help us. If you could do a little "guessing", the way you did when the Zenner kid was missing, maybe you could tell us where to look for this one.'

'Karen's no psychic,' said Mrs Connors. 'There's no way in the world that she can do what you're suggesting.'

'Maybe not. Then, again, who's to say for sure? What's there to lose by giving it a try?'

'It wouldn't work,' Karen told him. 'What I felt about Bobby was based on personal emotions. I wasn't just worried; I felt responsible. With this girl, Carla, that wouldn't be a factor. I've never even met her.'

'Will you just drive out to the house with me?' the

policeman asked her. 'If you met her mother – looked around her bedroom—'

'That's out of the question,' said Mrs Connors. 'Karen is not going to go to some strange house and play detective. The whole idea is ridiculous.'

The tone of voice was an echo from Karen's childhood. It evoked memories of the hundreds of past occasions on which decisions that pertained to her own welfare had been made without consulting her. The fact that her mother would, even today, assume the right to speak for her as though she were a puppet, sparked an unaccustomed flash of rebellion.

'Really, Mom,' she said testily, 'don't you think that's up to me?'

'I'll have her back in a couple of hours,' said Officer Wilson. 'If she doesn't get any feelings about Carla's whereabouts, then that will be the end of it.'

'And if she does – what then?' asked Mrs Connors. 'If, by some miracle, she *does* feel something, *does* manage somehow to point you in the right direction, she'll be marked for life as a freak.'

'That won't happen,' Officer Wilson assured her. 'Any information Karen provides for us will be confidential. It can only be classed as guesswork, so no source needs to be identified.' He turned back to Karen. 'Are you game to take a shot at this?'

'She is not,' Mrs Connors said firmly.

'Yes, I am,' Karen told them.

6

The Sanchez home was on the outskirts of Albuquerque in the rural area referred to by its residents as The Valley. The drive there took them along the edge of the Rio Grande.

The normally sluggish river, awakened from its winter lassitude by the heavy rains, was rushing brown and high. Along its banks the cottonwoods were budding, their leaves a pale, almost translucent green in the morning sunlight. Small nameless flowers, which would have been called weeds if they had popped up unexpectedly on people's lawns, dotted the landscape with splashes of purple and yellow, and the telephone wires running opposite the highway were strung with robins.

'I don't think I can do this,' said Karen.

'No problem,' Officer Wilson responded easily. 'If you can, great, but, if not, nothing's going to be lost.'

'Do you think that there are people who can, on request, like this? Even when they don't know the children they're looking for?'

'If I didn't think that, I wouldn't have asked you to try it.'

'Have you ever known someone like that?' Karen asked him.

'Yes, one. A good friend of mine. And I've heard about others.'

'The person you know – is he from Albuquerque?'

'It's a woman,' said Officer Wilson. 'Yes, she's from here. Her name's Anne Summers. She's had a lot of success in locating people, especially kids. I don't know why, but it seems like woman psychics are more tuned in to finding children than men are.'

'*Psychics.*' Karen repeated the word nervously. 'I'm not

a psychic. I'm a person who occasionally has lucky hunches. I don't know why you think that I'll have one now.'

'Maybe you won't.'

'If this Anne Summers is so talented,' Karen continued, 'why haven't the police asked *her* to find Carla Sanchez?'

'She's not available,' said Officer Wilson. 'She's working on a case in Texas.'

'A kidnapping?'

'A multi-kidnapping. Eight kids were taken from a day nursery.'

'I think I read about that in the paper,' Karen said. 'Wasn't it in one of the bigger cities, like Houston or somewhere?'

'In Dallas. Anne's been down there a couple of weeks now.'

They drove on for another mile or so, and then Officer Wilson turned the car off the highway on to a dirt road bordered on both sides by pasture land. Cows, some with newborn calves beside them, raised heads from their grazing to follow the car's progress along the rutted lane. The lushness of springtime closed in on them from all sides with walls of high grasses, green and thick and smelling of honeyed sunshine.

They crossed a bridge over an arroyo and made a second turn on to an even narrower road, which wound through a grove of poplars. When they drew to a stop at last, it was in front of a rundown adobe house with a rusted Chevrolet station wagon parked in the yard.

'We're here,' said Officer Wilson, shutting off the engine.

For a few moments they sat, unmoving. The absolute quiet of the countryside was hypnotic. The root of its stillness was in the absence of traffic noise, yet, once she had become adjusted to that, Karen found herself becoming aware of a number of gentler sounds. The clucking and scratching of chickens on the east side of the house. Birds, calling in the treetops. A tinkle of wind chimes, suspended somewhere out of sight in the branches above them.

Then, abruptly, the atmosphere was shattered by the crash of a screen door and a volley of wild barking. A small black and white terrier burst out of the house and came hurtling across the yard to throw itself full force against the side of the car. Close behind it, there followed a thin dark-haired woman, obviously of Spanish descent, who, in her way, seemed equally excited.

'Have you found her?' she called as she hurried towards them. 'Do you have my Carla? Is she OK?'

'Call off the dog, please, will you?' There was an edge to Officer Wilson's voice. 'I told you the last time I was out here that you ought to keep it tied.'

'Do you have Carla?' the woman persisted as though she had not heard him.

'No, not yet – and, look, I mean it, Mrs Sanchez – please, get that dog out of here. Shut it away someplace so we can get out and talk with you.'

'It's only a puppy,' said Karen. 'It doesn't look dangerous.'

'So – I don't like puppies. I don't like dogs – period – any shape, any size of them.'

'Come here, Coco.' The woman stooped and gathered up the leaping animal. 'I'll go put him in the toolshed, OK?'

'OK – fine. That'll be great. Just make sure the door's shut tight.'

They sat in silence while Mrs Sanchez carried the dog, still yapping, around the corner of the house. When she returned a few moments later with her arms empty, Officer Wilson opened the door and got out of the car.

'There's nothing new to report,' he said apologetically. 'I'm off duty today and not here on official business. I thought, though, it might be a good thing for you to talk to this friend of mine, Karen.'

'I don't need more talking,' said the woman. 'What I

need is my baby back. For a week now, she's been gone! For a week now, she's been off somewhere with that *hijo de puta*, crying for her mama, wanting to sleep at night in her own room. God knows what kind of place he has her in! You're the police! Why don't you find her?'

'These things take time,' said Officer Wilson. 'It's tough tracking down somebody who has no ties. At least, you know that the man is Carla's father. He's not going to do anything that's going to hurt her.'

'Carla needs to be home,' the woman said emphatically. 'She needs to be here with her mama. She needs to be in school.'

'We *are* going to find her, Mrs Sanchez. Believe me, we're doing the best we can.' He went around the car to the passenger's side and opened the door for Karen. 'This is Karen Connors. She's going to help us.'

'Help, how?' challenged Mrs Sanchez, regarding Karen suspiciously. 'She's not a police lady. She's just a young girl.'

'Karen finds children,' said Officer Wilson. 'Last week she found a boy who was missing. His parents were just as worried about him as you are about Carla. Karen closed her eyes and thought about him, and she was able to tell us where he was.'

Mrs Sanchez's expression altered slightly. Her dark eyes flickered with a sudden glint of something that could have been either hope or fear.

'*Una bruja?*' she questioned softly.

'No, not a witch, a "guesser". A special kind of guesser.'

'You guess right?' Mrs Sanchez asked Karen. 'You can guess where Carla is, and she will be there?'

'I can't make any promises,' said Karen. 'You mustn't count on anything. I knew the missing boy, but I don't know Carla. I don't even know what she looks like.'

'Her mother has a photograph,' said Officer Wilson. 'It's a recent one, taken just last fall.'

'It's her school picture,' Mrs Sanchez said. 'She looks so beautiful. Come inside, and I show you.'

The inside of the Sanchez home proved to be as unassuming as its mud brick exterior. The front room was sparsely furnished, containing only a sagging, overstuffed sofa, two worn chairs, and a large colour television set. The walls were plastered and painted white, and they were hung with an assortment of pictures depicting religious subject matter. The stars of the display seemed to be Jesus blessing children and the Virgin Mother in various attitudes of prayer.

On top of the TV, in a metallic ten-cent-store frame, there stood an eight-by-ten enlargement of a solemn-faced girl of grammar school age. Her eyes were dark and luminous, and her thick black hair fell almost to her waist. She was as pretty as her mother had indicated. She also looked shy and sweet and vulnerable. She did, indeed, appear to be a child who should be 'home with her mama'.

'It's her last school picture,' Mrs Sanchez said. 'This time she didn't blink. Last year when they took the picture her eyes were closed.'

'This picture is lovely,' said Karen.

'She's pretty, yes?'

'She's beautiful.'

'Could Karen see Carla's room?' asked Officer Wilson. 'If she could spend some time around Carla's things, she might be able to – well, to "guess" – a little better.'

'The best thing she likes now is her bike,' Mrs Sanchez told them. 'Her papa bought it for her when he got into town this last time.'

'Where is the bike?' the policeman asked her.

'It's not here now. They took it with them. I guess she wouldn't go without it. They didn't take anything else – not her clothes, not anything – but they took that new bike.'

'That's okay,' said Officer Wilson. 'It's the older things

that work the best for this. What about her toys and her favourite clothes? Are there things she's had since she was a baby?'

'Come, I'll show you,' said Mrs Sanchez.

Carla's bedroom was hardly more than a cubicle, but, perhaps for that very reason, there was a cosiness about it. There were Mickey Mouse curtains at the windows, and the narrow youth bed was covered with a hand-embroidered spread. On the pillow, there rested an obviously well-loved teddy bear who might once have been buttercup yellow but was now a shade more closely resembling apple cider. The only other furnishings consisted of a straight-backed chair and a chest of drawers with a mirror over it. On the walls there were framed pictures of the same religious subjects that were displayed in the living room.

Karen glanced helplessly about her.

'What am I supposed to do?'

'That's up to you,' Officer Wilson told her. 'What Anne does is sit in the room alone for a while and think about the person she wants to locate. She looks at the clothes and belongings. She touches them. She calls it "getting vibes".'

'You get vibes on Carla,' Mrs Sanchez said eagerly. 'We'll wait outside. When you get through, you come out and tell us where Carla and her papa are.' It was apparent from the altered tone of her voice that she was actually beginning to believe in the possibility of this hoped-for miracle's occurring.

'I'll try, but I can't guarantee anything,' said Karen. 'I can't believe – I mean, I just don't think—'

'Don't worry about it,' said Officer Wilson. 'Just think of it as an experiment. Either it works or it doesn't, OK?'

'OK,' said Karen.

But it *wasn't* OK. She realised that as soon as he and Mrs Sanchez had closed the door behind them, leaving her alone in Carla's tiny bedroom. The expression in the eyes of Carla's mother had been too abruptly trusting. The woman was desperate; she was ready to clutch at straws.

It's not fair, Karen thought resentfully. I didn't realise what I was getting into. That man had no right to put me in this position.

But, she was now committed. There was no way at this point that she would be able to get out of the predicament. She had to make an effort, and, as Officer Wilson had said, it would either work or it wouldn't. Actually, it wasn't totally inconceivable that she might be successful. After all, she *had* found Bobby. On that occasion, though, the vision had come of its own accord, springing effortlessly into her mind. To accept a spontaneous revelation was one thing. It was different to set out deliberately to try to create one.

'Look at the clothes,' Officer Wilson had suggested. Well, she could do that much at least. It would probably be as good a way to start as any.

Crossing the room to the closet, Karen opened the door and peered inside. There were only a few garments hanging from the crossbar – a winter parka, a couple of cotton school dresses, and, at the back, in a plastic dry-cleaner's bag, a white lace dress that had undoubtedly been worn by Carla at her First Communion.

Tentatively, Karen ran her fingers over the thin material of the parka. Carla must have spent some chilly days, she thought sympathetically. She touched the school clothes and then, with the uncomfortable feeling that she was intruding where she had no business, she took down the hanger that held the Communion dress.

Shoving back the protective covering, she lifted the folds of material to her face. With her eyes tightly closed, she tried to visualize Carla in the dress. It was easy to imagine what she must have looked like. With her huge eyes aglow and the soft mouth smiling, the child must have been as radiant as an angel.

Karen could imagine the picture, but she could not *see*

it. The face in her mind was only a reflection of the image in the photograph; there was no reality to it, as there had been with her vision of Bobby.

The starched lace was scratchy against her cheek, and the heavy odour of dry-cleaning chemicals assaulted her sinuses. It was obvious, Karen thought ruefully, that any 'vibes' she might get from Carla were not going to be found within the confines of this closet.

Karen replaced the hanger on the bar and carefully adjusted the dress so that it hung without wrinkles. Shoving the closet door closed, she went back over to the bed. She started to sit down, and then, on impulse, took off her shoes and stretched herself full length on top of the spread. Picking up the toy bear, she hugged it against her chest as Carla must often have done.

Again, she closed her eyes.

She lay there for a long time, waiting. Nothing happened. No sudden detailed vision came springing to greet her. The bed was soft and unevenly lumpy, and the bear smelled of chewing gum. Then, as moments passed, it began to take on another, less pleasant odour, like the faint, rank stench of mouldy dampness and rotting leaves.

The room was chilly – strangely so, since the day itself was not. Karen shivered and resisted the urge to slide in beneath the covers. The thick adobe walls of the Valley houses not only insulated against the cold of winter; they also did an effective job of keeping out the gentle warmth of springtime.

Cuddling the bear closer, she focused her thoughts determinedly on Carla. Somewhere she existed, a fragile, sweet-faced child in the company of the man who was her father. Where were they now? Karen asked herself, reaching out with her mind as far as she could, holding it open, waiting for an answer.

Time passed. Still, nothing happened.

At last, feeling ridiculous for having allowed herself to

be persuaded to attempt this feat, she got up from the bed, smoothed the spread and set the bear gently back on the pillow.

Then she went out into the living room to break the news to Carla's mother that the experiment had been a failure.

7

'I shouldn't have agreed to go there,' said Karen. 'I've never felt so dumb and foolish in all my life.'

They were driving back along the road by the river. It was a replay in reverse of the trip that they had made that morning, except that now the sun was high in the sky and the feeling of hopeful anticipation that had brightened the earlier trip was sadly missing.

'It was worth a try,' said Officer Wilson. 'Things aren't any worse now than they were before.' He paused, and then said, a bit too casually, 'About the dog—'

'The dog?' Karen repeated blankly.

'The mutt back there at the Sanchez place. You must have thought I acted pretty funny.'

'Lots of people don't like dogs,' said Karen.

'Yeah, but – well, here I am, a cop – I'm supposed to have it all together, right? And, then, I over-react like that. Well, the thing is—' He drew a deep breath. 'I got mauled by a Doberman when I was a kid. We were over visiting some friends of my parents, and my older brother and I were out running around in their backyard. The dog belonged next door. I guess it wasn't used to noisy kids. It went into some kind of frenzy and jumped the fence and tore right into me. It was a rotten experience. I've never been able to knock it.'

'How awful!' exclaimed Karen. 'Were you badly hurt?'

'My left arm was mangled. For a while, they thought they might have to amputate. It took two operations to get things fixed, and I've still got plenty of scars. The crazy thing was that Steve was closer to the fence than I was. The dog ran straight past him and threw itself on *me*.'

'Your brother wasn't bitten?'

'No, and he should have been. He pulled the dog off me

and never got so much as a nip. That's how it's always been with Steve, though. He's the family Wonder Boy – everything he touches turns to gold. He's currently at the top of his class in law school, married to a lady law student who could pass for Miss America. When they graduate, they're going into practice with my father. They've got the perfect kid, too; he could model for a baby food ad.' He took his left hand off the steering wheel to glance at his watch. 'Do you want to stop somewhere and pick up a sandwich? You never even got breakfast.'

'I'd like that.' Karen suddenly realised that she was, indeed, very hungry. 'Thanks, Officer Wilson.'

'Ron.'

'What?'

'My name's Ron. I'm off duty right now – I'm buying a pretty girl lunch – so, I'm Ron, okay? If we take the turnoff at the next intersection, we should run smack into a Burger King.'

'That sounds great,' said Karen. But – it *didn't*. 'No, let's not,' she contradicted herself. 'Let's stay on this road.'

'The eating places are all in closer to town,' Ron said.

'I'm sure I remember passing a McDonald's on our way out here.'

She heard herself making the statement with bewilderment. It was a blatant lie. There were no fast-food restaurants in this area.

Ron obviously knew this. He glanced at her sharply but did not comment.

The silence between them lengthened uncomfortably until Karen finally broke it.

'I don't know why I said that.'

'It doesn't matter.'

'I didn't want you to turn,' Karen said. 'I don't know why. I felt as though I had to come up with some sort of reason, so I said that – that stupid thing – about there being a McDonald's.'

'I'm not going to turn,' Ron said. 'I'll drive you anywhere you want to go.'

'It's not much further. A mile or so down this road is all, and then to the right. You'll be turning on to a dirt road like the one that led to the Sanchez place, but it will be narrower.'

She was issuing directions without reason. The instructions she was giving him made no more sense to her than they must to Ron. Karen knew little or nothing about the geography of the Valley. The few previous times that she had been out there had been back in her childhood when her mother had driven her out in the fall to buy apples and pumpkins. She had no memory of their having taken any detours on those occasions. The fruits and vegetables they had come for had been on prominent display on stands along the highway.

There was no explanation, either, for the tension that she was feeling. On one level, she did want Ron to keep on driving in the direction they were headed and to take the turnoff as she had indicated. On another, she wanted him to take her home. The feeling of apprehension might be ungrounded, yet it was increasing so rapidly that she was beginning to feel weak and a little nauseated.

Was what she was feeling simply a reaction to the pressure she had been under at the Sanchezes'? If so, why hadn't she experienced it sooner? In Carla's room, surrounded by the child's possessions, she had felt nothing. The white lace dress, which must surely have symbolised an important occasion in the little girl's life, had stirred no response from her whatsoever. The yellow bear, tattered with loving, had lain in her arms like a rock. If Carla, wherever she now might be, was missing her bear, was reaching out with her mind to recall its comforting softness, Karen had not felt any awareness of such longings. Bobby's terror she had experienced as though it were her own. Carla's emotions were not coming through to her at all.

Perhaps she isn't experiencing negative feelings, Karen thought suddenly. Maybe she *prefers* being with her father.

This was a possibility. Mrs Sanchez might have found her former husband selfish and irresponsible, but that didn't necessarily mean he would appear that way to an eight-year-old daughter. If she loved him and he was good to her, she might actually be happier in the care of an easy-going drifter than she had been with a strict and demanding mother.

More minutes passed. Then Karen said, 'Turn here.'

Ron obeyed immediately, pressing his foot to the brake and giving the steering wheel a quick twist to put the car on to a dirt road that was actually more of a hiking trail. Immediately, they seemed to have left civilisation behind them. Brush rose high on either side, cutting off the view of the highway, and branches reached out to claw at the fenders. Leaves flopped against the windshield, and the wheels spun and slid through mud-filled ruts.

'You're sure this is the turnoff you were thinking about?' Ron asked doubtfully. 'It's just an access to the river. It's bound to wind up as a dead end.'

'That's where we want to go,' Karen said. 'To the water.'

They continued to inch their way along as the trail wound further into the undergrowth. Eventually, as Ron had predicted, it terminated at the river, breaking through the brush and emerging into a sunlit hollow filled with wild flowers. Daisies bloomed there in abundance, thrusting white fringed heads triumphantly through matted, winter-browned grasses. Scattered among them, assorted other blossoms in no-name brands darted out in unexpected places, like bright-coloured remnants from a flower maker's closet. Birds were singing, not chirping and calling but trilling happily, and the gurgle of the rushing river was as joyous as human laughter.

The place was beautiful. And it was terrible.

Karen did not want to be there.

'You were right,' she said. 'It's just a dead end with nothing here. Let's go back.'

Ron shook his head. 'There must be some reason you wanted to come here.'

'There's nothing to see.'

'There might be. We'll never know unless we take a look.'

Without giving her time to respond, he shut off the engine and opened the door on the driver's side. The chorus of bird voices became louder and the sound of the river more uproarious.

Karen's head began to throb.

'I don't feel good,' she whispered. 'I want to go home.'

'I know.' Ron's voice was surprisingly gentle. 'The truth is, kid, I don't feel so hot myself.'

'Please, can't we leave?'

'I'm afraid not. Not until this is finished.'

Karen opened the door on her own side and got out slowly. Her legs felt weak, and her stomach was churning. Was it possible that a short time ago she had actually felt like eating? Now the mere idea of food was revolting to her.

The sun was warm on her arms and the back of her neck, yet she found that she was shivering uncontrollably.

'Where to now?' Ron asked softly.

Karen gestured blindly off to the right towards a path that led along the riverbank. Ron took a step in that direction and then turned back and reached for her hand. Numbly, Karen let him take and hold it. To her surprise, she found that his was trembling.

After another few steps, their eyes were caught by a metallic glitter at the hollow's edge. It was the chrome handlebars of a child's bicycle, which had been carefully propped against the trunk of a giant cottonwood.

'Is it hers?' Karen asked.

'I can't be sure. It's the right size to be.'

'It's new,' Karen said. 'You can tell that by looking at it. The paint doesn't have any scratches.'

'On our way back I'll stop and check out the serial number.'

He released her hand so that they could walk in single file on the narrowing trail. It twisted away from the river to manoeuvre around a tree trunk and then dipped abruptly to a pebble-covered beach. Flat rocks, black and gleaming, extended into the river and broke the stream of the current so that it swirled chaotically around them, tossing froth about like confetti.

On the beach, set well back from the water, there lay a pair of sandals.

'You can go back to the car now, Karen,' Ron said.

She heard him, but there was no way at this point that she could have moved from the spot on which she was planted. Her eyes were riveted on the shoes.

They came from K-Mart. The knowledge was as absolute as though she had been there at the time of their purchase. She knew those shoes. She could feel the cheap metal buckles in her fingers as the child who owned them struggled to get them open. The right one came easily, but the left was harder. She gave it a quick, impatient jerk, and the flimsy, imitation leather strap came loose from the sole.

Dios mio! Mama would be mad about that! 'Shoes do not grow on trees!' she would say, because that was what she always said. 'Shoes cost money! If that father of yours would send some support money—' *But he bought me a bicycle!* 'You need a bike like you need a hole in your head. You need school clothes!' *School is almost over. I won't need school clothes in the summer!*

Karen closed her eyes in a frantic attempt to shut out the scene, but it would not leave her. If anything, it seemed to intensify. She could feel the jagged pebbles beneath the soles of winter-tender feet. Water splashed, cold, upon her ankles.

How lovely to have it springtime! In another six weeks or so the river would grow shallow and tepid, oozing dutifully along its wellworn route, pausing at extended intervals to languish, heavy and motionless, stultified by the heat of the blazing summer sun. It was no fun then. It was boring. Not like today, when it surged young and wild and filled with spirit.

The mud squished deliciously between her toes. The water was like liquid ice. Her feet were becoming numb, but that was all right; that was part of the adventure.

The current was stronger than she had anticipated. Her jeans were getting wet now. She had rolled them up to her knees, but one of the pant legs kept slipping down. If she shoved them both higher, maybe she could make it all the way out to the largest of the rocks without getting sopping. In the summer that particular rock stuck up a good ten inches above the water, but today it could barely be seen above the surface.

She wondered if her bike was all right, sitting back there in the clearing all by itself. Perhaps she should go back and check on it. The path was so narrow, she had been afraid to wheel the bike along it for fear the bushes would scratch the paint. But, then, who was there to steal it? Nobody ever came here except for her. Nobody knew about this special, private wading spot – not her mama, not her school friends, not anybody.

When I grow up, I will have my husband build our house here. I will take our children wading—

'Karen, stop it!' Strong hands gripped her shoulders, shaking her fiercely. 'Open your eyes! You've got to come out of it! You can't do this to yourself!'

'She fell,' Karen whispered. 'Off the big rock. She was bending over, trying to get the legs of her jeans pulled up. The rock was slippery—'

'Open your eyes!'

She did, and the glare of the sun struck her full in the

face like an electric shock. Its brilliance exploded upon her, shattering the vision.

'She fell,' Karen repeated. 'I saw her fall.'

'I know. I believe you.' Ron's face was pale. 'I *saw* you seeing her. You looked like – like you were going to keel over or something.'

'Can we go home now?' Karen asked him.

'Sure,' Ron said. 'Sure, we can.' He released his grip on her shoulders but kept his hands poised at either side of them as though afraid she might not be able to keep her balance. 'Are you OK?'

'I don't know,' Karen said.

'Do you want to sit down?'

'Not here. I want to get out of here.'

'We'll leave in one minute. First, I've got to get the shoes.'

He left her standing on the path while he scrambled down the short, steep incline to the beach. He bent to pick up the sandals, and when he straightened and turned, Karen was not surprised to see that the strap of the left one had been pulled away from the sole and was flapping loose in his hands exactly as she had envisioned it.

8

They had barely reached the car when the mental exhaustion, frightening, yet familiar, came rolling in upon her like a gigantic wave from some dark and syrupy sea.

Karen struggled to keep her eyes open and her mind functioning. Ron was talking to her. She could see his lips moving and was aware of the sound of his voice, but the words themselves slid past her in a meaningless jumble of disjointed syllables as though they were being spoken in a foreign tongue.

The knowledge was undeniable. Carla Sanchez was dead. Somewhere in that rushing river, there was the body of a barefooted, blue-jeaned child. The bright new bike would go unridden; the yellow bear unhugged. The dresses in the closet of the tiny bedroom would be taken from hangers and given to Goodwill. The portrait on the television set in the living room would be enshrined for ever now, no longer just a photograph, but the last school picture – the *final* picture – 'the way Carla looked the last year of her life'.

Mrs Sanchez would show it to everyone who entered the house. She would speak in past tense, her pride shrouded in pain. *She was so beautiful, my Carla!*

'How could I do it?' Karen whispered. 'How *could* I!'

'You didn't do anything,' Ron's voice assured her, the words lapping against her ears and slipping away again like ripples in a pond. 'It was already done. It happened a week ago. All you did was show me where it occurred.'

'You said she was with her father!'

'We thought she was. It was so logical; her dad came to visit – he left – the kid was gone. It fitted so well.'

'There's no proof that it didn't happen that way,' said Karen. 'Like you told my mother, this was only "guesswork". It doesn't count for anything. It's not as though Carla's been found.'

'She will be,' Ron said with grim certainty.

'I won't go back,' Karen told him. 'I won't ever go back to that terrible place.'

'You won't have to,' Ron said. 'Your part is over. What you've got to do now is put this behind you.'

She was aware that he was continuing to talk to her, but his words seemed to be coming from farther and farther away, muffled and lost in the haze of fatigue that was enveloping her. She gave in to the weight of her eyelids, and when she managed once again to force them open, she found that the car had come to a stop.

'You're home,' Ron said. 'I'll come in with you and help you tell your parents.'

'They're not here,' Karen said. 'My dad's playing golf, and Mom's car isn't in the driveway. She's probably gone shopping or something.'

'Do you want me to wait with you until they get back?'

'No,' Karen said. 'I'll be fine.'

'I know how rotten you're feeling. I don't like to drop you off like this with no one home.'

'I don't need anybody.'

Please, go away. Go drag the river or whatever policemen do when they're looking for bodies.

'I'm tired,' Karen said. 'I just want to lie down.'

'Well, if you're sure you'll be OK—'

'I'm sure.'

She opened the door and got out of the car, feeling dizzy and uncoordinated, as if her brain had somehow become disconnected from her body. As she made her way up the pathway, the house appeared to be receding as she approached it, like a desert mirage. It was only when she turned and looked back at the car that she was able to see that she had been making progress.

In this dreamlike state, she continued walking, realising

at some level of her consciousness that the dulled condition she was experiencing was her body's way of cushioning itself against shock.

When she at last did reach the house, she discovered that the door was locked. Though this was only to be expected, it was all that she could do to keep from bursting into tears. The rummage through her purse to locate her house key loomed as one more next to impossible hurdle to clear before she could set the dreadful morning behind her.

It seemed a million years before her fingers finally closed upon the key, and when she tried to fit it into the keyhole her hand was shaking. She wrestled with the key and then with the doorknob, painfully conscious of the fact that Ron was watching from the car, ready to rejoin her at any indication that help might be needed.

Go away! she wanted to scream at him. *Can't you understand that after this experience, I never want to think about you again!*

At last, the knob turned and the door swung open. Karen stepped quickly into the hallway and shoved the door closed behind her. She felt a sense of overwhelming relief as she heard the click of the latch falling into place.

On the far side of the entrance hall, there rose the staircase, extending endlessly upward as though it led to the very gates of eternity. Karen approached it with grim determination, making each of the steps a separate challenge: *There are fifteen still ahead of me – now there are fourteen – now only thirteen.* By the time she had reached the second-floor hallway, she was staggering under the weight of such exhaustion that she could barely keep from sinking to the floor.

Resisting that temptation, she continued on down the hall and entered her bedroom. It was bright with afternoon sunlight, and the gentle blue walls glowed softly like sections of sky. Karen closed the door and crossed the room to the bed. The rumpled sheets and mussed covers were a reminder of her hasty morning exodus. The spread lay tossed on the floor, its petal-sprinkled surface smiling up at her like a woodland clearing dotted with wild flowers. The shade of the porcelain lamp on the bedside table echoed the pattern – *flowers, flowers by a river*. The costumed dolls that lined the shelf on the far wall seemed to run together into a blur of blended shapes and colours. The only one who stood out clearly was clothed in a white lace dress that might have been a First Communion gown.

'Put this behind you,' Ron had commanded. How easy that was to say and how impossible to accomplish!

I will never forget this day as long as I live.

Karen threw herself down on to the tumbled bed and closed her eyes. As if on summons, the backs of her lids sprang to life like twin movie screens displaying a sequence of overlapping visions. A newborn baby, red and gleaming, let out its first shrill cry. That same baby, cheeks grown rounded, nuzzled contentedly at its mother's breast. A toddler in a damp and drooping diaper staggered triumphantly across the front room of a small adobe home. 'She's walking! *La niña* is walking!' And then – a birthday party! 'What's in the package from Nana? A yellow Teddy! *Mira*, Carla, *mira! Mira el bonito oso de trapo!*'

I will not see! I will not look!

But there was no way to avoid looking, for scene followed scene so rapidly that it was no longer possible to separate one from another. The child grew taller. The baby-soft hair gave way to rich, dark locks that fell thick about her shoulders. She rocked her dolls. She played with blocks. She gathered eggs from the henhouse for her mother. Her father took her to an amusement park, where she ate tacos and cotton candy and washed them down with orange soda pop. '*Idiota!*' shouted the mother. 'What do you expect when you feed her junk like that? Of course, she throws up on the ferris wheel!' Carla cried. She had not meant to get sick and make her mama angry.

There was heavy snow that winter. There was ice in the river, and the wind blew very cold. Spring came, and summer, and autumn; leaves spun crazily from green to gold to brown in one dizzying instant.

'Stop,' Karen whispered, or tried to whisper, but the images kept coming, piling one on top of another, faster and faster, as though a projector had gone mad in some deep centre point of her brain.

Carla was in school now, and her father was gone. 'We will do without him fine,' her mother assured her. He was not there for the First Communion, but he sent Carla a card with five dollars in it and no return address on the envelope. The yellow bear fell into the toilet and was rescued. Mama boiled it to kill the germs. The school picture was taken, and Carla's eyes were closed. Carla felt so sad about the picture that Mama made new Mickey Mouse curtains for her bedroom and Nana embroidered a bedspread. 'Happy birthday, Carlita! Blow out the candles!' 'But there are eight of them. I'm only seven.' 'There is one to grow on. Don't you want to grow up big?' Another school picture – 'Oh, that's a good one!'

That winter was milder – frost on the panes of the windows – *luminarias* at Christmas. Another spring, and the father was home for a visit. 'Go see what is in the back of the truck for you.' 'A bicycle! Oh, I love it! I love it! Thank you, Papa!' 'You need a bike like you need a hole in your head! You need school clothes!' 'School is almost over, Mama. All I need are sandals.' 'Shoes do not grow on trees.'

Papa was gone again. He took Carla out for a ride in his truck before he left, and they stopped at a drive-in for ice cream. 'One of these days I'll have you come stay with me. First, I have to find a job. Up in Vegas there's a lot of work opening up. That's where I'm headed. When I find me a job and a place to live, then I'll send you a plane ticket.'

He let her off in front of the house and kissed her

goodbye. After he drove away, Carla stood, staring at the house, thinking about her mother inside, waiting for her. She would ask questions. 'What did your papa say to you? Is he going to start sending money? Does he have a lady friend? Does he want to take you away with him?'

It's not her business what Papa tells me. I don't have to go inside. Mama doesn't even know I'm home. I can take my bike and go to the river. It's so much fun in springtime. The water's so fast and cold, and there are so many flowers. I can go wading—

No more! Karen screamed silently. I won't see the rest – I won't.

She struggled frantically to thrust the images from her, but they were now no longer visions, but dreams. The nightmare rush of water filled her ears. Clutching desperately at the last thin thread of consciousness, she felt it slipping away. Icy currents closed upon her, and, tumbling, choking, gasping, she was swept into oblivion.

When she awoke, something had mysteriously altered. The room was still bright with sunlight, and a chorus of bird voices was twittering in the elm tree outside the window, and beyond that sound there came another – the thin, sweet chime of bells from the Methodist church over on Copper Avenue.

What in the world? Karen asked herself in bewilderment. Then the realisation struck her – she had slept straight through from Saturday afternoon until Sunday morning!

Why hadn't her parents wakened her for dinner? Or had they tried and been unsuccessful? She could tell from the aching stiffness of her body that she had not changed position all night. She was still fully clothed except for her shoes; someone had removed those, and the spread that had been on the floor at the foot of the bed had been pulled up to cover her.

For a long time she lay, listening to the distant chimes,

trying to tell herself that today was simply another Sunday, that yesterday had been just another Saturday, that the soul-chilling dreams had been just that – horrible dreams. But, the weight at the pit of her stomach told her something different. What had happened the day before had been real. She had been a part of a tragedy, and from now until the end of her life, *it* would be part of *her*.

If she had been able to force herself back to sleep she would have, but that form of escape was to be denied her. Although weariness lay heavy upon her, her mind was clear and functioning. Eventually, when the bells had ceased their chiming, she got out of bed and went into the bathroom to brush her teeth. To her surprise, the face in the mirror above the sink, though a little pale, was not noticeably different from the face she was used to seeing there. She was still Karen Connors, still eighteen years old, blonde, brown-eyed, acceptably pretty. On the surface, at least, she had come through this experience unscathed.

When she went downstairs, she found her parents in the kitchen, drinking coffee. The morning paper was spread on the table between them so that the first thing that met Karen's eyes as she entered the room was the screaming black headline: 'Body of Missing Child Found in River'. Directly beneath this there was a two-column, black and white reproduction of Carla's school picture.

'It was on the ten o'clock news,' her father said by way of greeting. 'We didn't see any reason to wake you up to tell you. This morning seemed soon enough for you to know.'

'They found her so quickly,' Karen said softly.

'They had help,' said Mrs Connors. 'Here – read all about yourself. You're an instant celebrity.'

'What do you mean?' Karen asked, startled. 'Ron said my name wouldn't be given out to anybody.'

'It's too bad you didn't get the same promise from Mrs Sanchez,' her mother said. 'She didn't feel any hesitancy

72

about talking. Here's the article. Go ahead – read it. You can be sure that by this time everybody else in town has.'

Karen sat down at the table and reluctantly pulled the paper towards her. She read the story and found nothing in it that was a surprise to her. The body of eight-year-old Carla Sanchez, missing since 20 April, had been found at six forty-five the previous evening, caught in a log jam in the Rio Grande, four miles east of the girl's south Valley home. Police were led to investigate this area of the river on the advice of a young psychic, the child's mother had told reporters. The psychic, a teenage girl named Karen Connors, had been brought to the family home by a police officer that morning.

Lorenzo Sanchez, the dead girl's father, had phoned his former wife from Las Vegas upon hearing a report of their daughter's death on his car radio.

'It was a terrible shock,' he was quoted as saying.

There was no evidence of foul play.

'Carla apparently decided to go wading, slipped, and was caught by the current,' said police officer Ronald Wilson, who directed the search for the child's body.

The youthful psychic, daughter of Mr and Mrs Paul Connors, 1872 Verona Avenue, was not available for questioning, her parents had told reporters.

'You mean, reporters called here last night?' asked Karen. 'How did they know where I lived?'

'They probably called every Connors in the book,' said her mother. 'Newspaper people are trained to ferret out information. This is exactly what I warned you about. I wish to heaven you would occasionally listen.'

'And *I* wish that somebody would tell me what this is all about,' Karen's father said. 'Since when is our daughter hiring herself out as a psychic?'

'I didn't hire myself out,' Karen said. 'This policeman, Ron Wilson, who was over at the Zenners', came by the house yesterday and asked if I would help him.'

'That much I know,' her father said. 'Your mother told me about it. What I don't understand is why you would want to get involved in a situation that has nothing to do with you.'

'I didn't ask to get involved,' Karen told him. 'Ron came to *me*. He asked me—'

The telephone rang.

Mrs Connors shoved back her chair and got up from the table. She picked up the receiver of the kitchen extension.

'Hello? Yes, this is the Connors' residence . . . No, no, she isn't . . . No, I don't know where you can reach her.' There was a long moment of silence. 'No,' Mrs Connors said, 'I don't think she can do that. Where is it you're calling from? How could you possibly – ? . . . Oh, I see. I didn't realise.'

There was another pause, more extended than the first one.

'I'm terribly sorry,' Karen's mother said at last. 'That just won't be possible. The story was incorrect. The mother was under terrible stress at the time she made the statement . . . Yes, I'm sure you are . . . Yes, I can imagine what that must be like . . . I *am* sorry. I hope they find her soon. Goodbye.'

She replaced the receiver on the hook and turned back to the table.

'That call was from New Jersey. The story has been picked up by the wire services. People on the East Coast are reading about it over lunch right now. In another hour, the ones in California will be reading it over breakfast.'

'What was the call about?' asked Karen.

'The man on the phone has a fifteen-year-old daughter who's been missing since February. Her boyfriend disappeared at the same time, and they think the two kids are together. He wants to know if the psychic in our family can tell him where they are.'

The phone began to shrill again.

'That thing's been ringing ever since I woke up this morning,' said Mr Connors. 'In fact, that's *why* I woke up. Either we leave it off the hook, or I'm going to the office.'

'But, it's Sunday,' Karen's mother objected. 'And you weren't home yesterday at all.'

'So what if it's Sunday? There's always paperwork to do.' He turned to Karen. 'Go ahead and answer it. You know it has to be for you.'

'We could just let it ring,' Karen said tentatively.

'No, we can't,' said her father. 'If you don't pick it up, they'll hang up and dial again. It's been that way since dawn.'

The call was from Tim.

'Gary just phoned me,' he said. 'He was talking to Lisa. She says there's a story about you in the paper.'

'It's not about *me*,' Karen said. 'It's about a little girl who died in a drowning accident. My name is mentioned in it, that's all.'

'I guess it must be! Gary said it makes you out to be some sort of fortune-teller who finds dead bodies and hauls them out of rivers. Christ, Karen, what *happened* yesterday?'

'It wasn't what you're saying,' said Karen. 'I never actually saw the child. I wasn't there when they found her.'

'But the paper says you told the police where to look for her!'

'It was like it was with Bobby,' Karen told him. 'I – had this feeling.'

'You had a *feeling* some Mexican kid was drowned in the river?'

'It does sound crazy,' Karen admitted.

'How could you know a thing like that? What were you doing out there anyway? Were those people friends of yours?'

'No,' Karen said. 'Look, Tim, can't we drop it? It was an awful experience. I'd really like to forget it.'

'Forget it!' Tim repeated incredulously. 'After that newspaper story? That part about you being a psychic – that's what Gary kept quoting. He kept asking me if you really do that kind of stuff.'

'And what did you tell him?'

'I said, no, of course not; that the paper must have got your name mixed up with somebody else's.'

'That was the right thing to say.'

'What do you mean by that?' Tim demanded. 'Is it true or isn't it? You're not trying to tell me you're really a psychic, are you?'

'What I'm trying to tell you is that I don't want to talk about it any more,' Karen said.

She hung up the phone.

9

The rest of the spring was hideous.

It should have been lovely. It was the prettiest spring that Karen could ever remember. The early rains had done their job well, leaving lawns glistening vibrant green like hundreds of miniature golf courses and pansy faces smiling up at the edges of walkways. As if on cue, on the first day of May, forsythia bushes in what seemed to be every yard in town exploded into golden glory and bright splashes of tulips burst forth in front-yard gardens.

And the Prom was coming – and Graduation—

And letters.

The letters began arriving three days after the story appeared in the paper. The timing wasn't surprising, Karen told herself. Those people who read the article and reacted immediately would spend a day working on their letters and would then mail them. The Postal Service would take a day for transportation and another for delivery. What was more difficult to understand was why each day's load of mail was heavier than that of the day before, and how, in a world filled with so much beauty, there could be so much pain.

Each afternoon when she arrived home from school, she was greeted by a mailbox filled with desperation. She could almost feel the agony of the contents burning her hands when she handled the unopened envelopes.

'How can there be so many missing children?' she exclaimed incredulously to her mother. 'Why aren't the police out there finding them?'

'Some of them undoubtedly don't want to be found,' said Mrs Connors. 'A lot are probably runaways.'

'But what about the preschoolers? What about the babies – where do *they* go? One letter yesterday was from a woman who said her ten-month-old son disappeared out of a cart in the supermarket. She turned her back for a minute to pick out some melons, and when she turned around again, he was gone. She wants me to come to Montana. She says she'll send my plane fare, and if I find the baby, she'll sell her house and pay me everything she gets for it.'

'Poor woman!'

'I can't go,' said Karen. 'I can't face such a thing.'

'Of course you can't,' her mother said firmly. 'You'd have to be crazy even to consider it.'

'If it happened again, like it did with Carla – if I *did* find that child, and something terrible had happened – I couldn't bear it.'

'Write back and tell her it was all a mistake,' Mrs Connors said. 'Tell her the reporter got the information wrong.'

'That's what I was planning.'

She answered that letter as she did the rest of them, in short, apologetic sentences which soon became such a form reply that she could have written them in her sleep. The phone calls were harder to deal with. Those came complete with live, human voices, some frantic and edged with hysteria, others heavy with worry of such long duration that it had settled into dragging despair. All were sparked momentarily with hope, however, as they questioned eagerly, 'Are you the girl I read about in the Sarasota *Herald Tribune*?' – or 'in the Detroit *Times*?' – or 'in the Morenci *Observer*?'

'Yes,' Karen would tell them, 'but the story was misleading. I can't do anything to help you. I'm not what you think I am.'

But the voices would not be silenced. The people who owned them plunged stubbornly onward, pouring out their stories in torrents of uncontrollable emotion. They needed to talk, to share their agony, to ask again and again as though they had not heard or were unwilling to comprehend the meaning of her response, 'Where do you think my boy could be?' or 'If this were your little sister, where would you look for her?'

'I don't know,' Karen told and retold them.

She said the same thing at school. It seemed that the entire student body had either read the newspaper article or seen the report on television. Even her teachers seemed fascinated by the subject. Her English teacher, Mrs Ellsworth, held her after class one day to ask whether there could be 'any truth in that incredible story', and the principal, Mr Daugherty, stopped her in the hall to inquire in an amused voice what it was like to find one's self 'an overnight celebrity'.

'Just awful,' Karen said. 'It was all a big mistake.'

'Or maybe it wasn't. Have you heard the term *yellow journalism*? Some reporters will write anything just to cause a sensation.'

Most people did believe her, or, at least, appeared to.

Tim was the exception.

'Don't give me that,' he told her.

They were parked in front of the Connors' home after a movie date. The setting was romantic. The night air smelled of flowers, and the sky, viewed through the front windshield of Tim's Pontiac, was deep and clear and studded with stars.

Tim's right arm lay along the back of the seat, and his hand cupped Karen's shoulder, but his voice was gruff with irritation.

'Look, I'm not some nosy stranger – I'm me, Tim – the guy you're going with. We're supposed to play straight with each other.'

'How straight?' asked Karen. 'What is it exactly that you want me to tell you?'

'The truth, that's what,' Tim said, 'not this stuff about everything's having been a mistake. On the phone you said it was "like it was with Bobby". So, how *was* it with Bobby? How did you know he was in my car?'

'I heard the trunk lid slam.'

'Bull!' Tim exploded. 'You couldn't have heard anything. You were back in the kitchen with the baby.'

'What are you bringing this up for now?' Karen asked him. 'At the time it didn't seem to matter to you. That next Monday at school, you never asked me anything about it.'

'I was too shook up at that point to worry about something like that. All I cared about right then was whether or not the Zenners were going to press charges. They could have, you know; their kid almost suffocated. Now, though, I'm thinking differently. Suddenly, we have this other thing happening. There's another kid missing, and this one is dead, and her mother says you're the one who found her. Can you blame me for wanting to know what's going on?'

'No,' Karen admitted reluctantly. She paused. 'The truth is, I don't know myself exactly. I honestly don't know how I did it. It just seemed to happen.'

'Like how?' Tim prodded.

'It was like seeing pictures,' Karen told him. 'That time with Bobby, I saw him in a sort of box. I smelled sweat and grease, and then I felt motion. Suddenly it came to me that the box must be in a car.'

'Far out!' Tim exclaimed softly.

'So "far out" I thought I was going crazy. But the feelings kept getting stronger. Mr Zenner got angry. He was upset enough, he said, without having to listen to premonitions. Then I told Ron Wilson.'

'That cop?'

'Yes, and he believed me. He'd had experience with this sort of thing before, he said. He has a friend who's a—' The word did not come easily. She forced herself to speak it. 'He has a friend who's a psychic.'

'This whole thing blows me away!' Tim shook his head

in amazement. 'It's like a science fiction movie. What I can't understand, though, is why you're trying to cover it up. This could make you famous!'

'I don't want to be famous,' said Karen. 'It was horrible finding out what happened to Carla. It wasn't as though there was something I could do that might have saved her. What had happened was already over. I had to watch and know that. I had to feel the things she had felt and share what she'd remembered.'

'What do you mean by that?'

'You've heard about how people's lives flash before them when they're drowning? I used to wonder if that was true, and, if it was, how anybody would know it.' She shook her head. 'Well, *I* know it now, and it *is* true. I never want to drown, Tim. It's a horrible way to die.'

She could feel his bewilderment. The arm around her shoulders had stiffened, and his hand had begun to move gently up and down her arm as though it were stroking an overexcited kitten.

'You were pretty upset,' Tim said. 'Of course, you had a right to be. Stuff like this would upset anybody. But, what you said just now about experiencing that girl's *memories* — that couldn't happen, Karen. It had to be something you imagined.'

'I did experience them,' Karen insisted.

'You were under a ton of stress. You could have hallucinated. That's possible, isn't it?'

There was nothing to be gained by arguing.

'It's possible, I guess.'

'Still, you've got to have psychic ability, or you couldn't have found her. I've read about people who could do that kind of thing. There was one lady who was written up in *Newsweek* back when all those black kids were getting murdered in Georgia. The police called her in to help with the investigation.'

'Maybe so. I don't remember.' Karen shifted position.

Her shoulders were beginning to ache under the weight of his arm. 'I'd better go in now. We've got school in the morning, and finals are coming up.'

'Did you have to remind me?' Tim muttered. 'I've been trying to pretend to myself that they're already over. You know, in a lot of schools seniors get excused from finals. The principals figure that eleven and a half years of that type of torture is enough for anybody.'

'Try explaining that to Mr Daugherty. I don't think you'll get very far.' Karen lifted her face expectantly for his goodnight kiss.

His lips pressed down upon hers lightly, almost absent-mindedly, as though his thoughts were somewhere else. She could not read his expression in the darkness, but she could sense that he was trying to decide about something.

'What is it?' she asked.

'What do you mean, "What is it"?'

'There's something you're wondering whether you ought to say.'

'The girl really is a mind-reader!'

The words were flippant, but there was something in the tone in which they were spoken that gave them more importance than they seemed to warrant.

'You're right,' Tim continued. 'I was thinking about the American Lit. exam. We've covered so much material this semester that Mrs Ellsworth could throw just about anything at us on the test.'

'You know there'll be Emerson, and there's sure to be Whitman. She'll probably ask for quotes from *Leaves of Grass*.'

'Or from something by Poe. Or by Emily Dickinson. Or, she could decide to centre the whole exam in the Twentieth Century with poets like Creeley and Rich and Ginsberg.'

'She could, I guess.'

'It'll be a bitch to study for.'

'All of her tests are.' She wished that she could see his face. 'What are you driving at?'

'Well,' Tim said slowly, 'I was wondering about this psychic thing you do. Do you suppose you could use it to – to sort of – picture the question sheet?'

'Picture the question sheet?' Karen echoed without comprehension. 'You mean, you want me to—' Suddenly, she realised what it was that he was asking. 'Oh, Tim, no! I couldn't do that! I can't tell in advance what the questions on a test will be.'

'How do you know you can't? Have you ever tried?'

'No,' Karen admitted, 'but I know I couldn't do it. It's people I tune in to, not things.'

'You could tune in to Mrs Ellsworth. She'll be thinking up the questions. If you were able to get into Carla's mind when you'd never even seen her – when she wasn't even *living* any longer – why can't you get into the mind of a teacher you've been seeing almost every day all semester long?'

'I just can't, that's all,' said Karen. 'And if I could, I wouldn't. This isn't the sort of thing you play games with.'

'Who's talking about game playing? I'm suggesting a scientific experiment.'

'Doing parlour tricks? Picking minds? You call that scientific? That's like picking pockets.'

'Aren't you even a little bit curious about how far you can go with this?' Tim asked her.

'No, I'm not,' said Karen. 'I've told you, it's over. I've put it behind me. Bobby's been found – Carla is gone – and the one thing in the world I want to do right now is to forget about both of them.'

'Now, look, Karen, you've got to face the fact—'

'I don't have to face anything,' Karen said adamantly. 'I didn't ask for this – this "gift" or whatever you want to call it – and, if I don't want to use it, that ought to be *my* decision. The last few weeks have been absolute hell. I never want to go through anything like them again. I just want everything to go back to the way it was.'

'OK! OK! I was only making a suggestion.' Tim lifted his arm from her shoulders and leaned across her to pull the handle of the door on the passenger's side. 'So, go ahead and get out! Go inside and study! Memorise every poem in the whole blasted lit. book! Pretend you're just like everybody else, if that's what you want to do. But, you've got to know it's pretending. If you're so tuned in to this far-out stuff that you can listen to a dead kid's *memories*—'

'You said I was hallucinating!'

'I'm not so sure any more. That business about knowing what a drowning girl was thinking – that's no crazier than any of the rest of it, when you come right down to it. It's weird, sure, but then the whole thing's weird.'

'And it takes a weird person to do weird things – that's what you're thinking, isn't it?' Karen challenged.

'I didn't say that.'

'You didn't have to!'

'So maybe it is what I'm thinking. You're the one who said it, though; I didn't.' Tim's voice was sharp with exasperation. 'This conversation is getting us nowhere. Let's call it a night, OK?'

'That's what I suggested twenty minutes ago.'

Karen shoved open the door and got out of the car.

'Don't forget your purse,' Tim said coldly.

'I didn't intend to.'

She leaned back in and groped along the seat until her hands closed upon the strap. She half expected that Tim might reach out to her, that he might try to take her hand and draw her towards him in an effort to erase the animosity that had arisen between them.

But this did not occur.

He was angry. Very angry. Well, so was she!

Karen slammed the car door hard and walked briskly

across the lawn to the house. Her parents had left on the outside light for her, and a cloud of moths swarmed around it, hurling themselves against the illuminated glass globe in a mindless frenzy. Their soft brown wings fluttered against her face as she fumbled through her purse for her house key.

In the street behind her, the engine of Tim's car sprang into life. He wasn't even going to wait to see that she was safely inside.

He's going to leave me, Karen told herself numbly. Not just for tonight, but for ever.

For one wild moment she considered turning and running back to him. 'Please, wait!' she would call. 'I'll try to get you the questions!'

Perhaps she would actually find she was able to do it. If so, who would be hurt by that? Not Mrs Ellsworth; she wouldn't even know about it. Since she didn't grade on a curve, the marks of the other students would not be affected. It would be, as Tim had said, just a scientific experiment.

But the test was not the issue. Tim's anger was surface anger that would blow over. They'd had arguments before, and she had finally come to realise that his bursts of temper never lasted. The fight they'd had at the Zenners' the morning of Bobby's disappearance had been far worse than this one, yet Tim had arrived for their date that evening as though nothing had happened.

No, this was different. This went deeper. Beneath the façade of anger there lay another emotion, one Tim would never admit to, but one that she could sense.

It was *fear*.

Fear of the unknown – of the unnatural. Fear of something or someone who was 'weird'.

Karen found the key, thrust it into the lock, and opened the door. The sound of the television came surging to meet her, just as it always did when she had been out for the evening.

She closed and relocked the door and went down the hall to the den. Her father was seated in his usual chair in front of the TV set, his eyes fastened to the screen.

'I'm home,' announced Karen when it became apparent that he didn't see her there in the doorway.

'Oh – hi!' He tore his gaze from the picture and gave her a nod of greeting. 'Your mother's gone up to bed already. She has another of her headaches. How was the movie?'

'All right, I guess. Not the best I've ever seen.'

'You had a phone call,' her father told her. 'Somebody named Ron something or other. He left his number. He said he'd like for you to call him when you get a chance.'

'I don't want to,' said Karen.

'Well, don't, then. There's no law that says you have to return a phone call.'

'He's not somebody I want to talk to,' said Karen. 'If he calls again, please, tell him I've nothing to say to him.'

When she slept that night, she did not dream at all.

She woke in the morning feeling empty and untroubled, scooped out and washed clean of all emotion.

It was over – all of it was over. Gratefully, she realised that there were to be no more nightmares. If Tim had been lost along with them, then that must be accepted. It was a hard-won lesson, but she had now learned it. Love meant losing. Joy meant pain. Investing oneself in others brought nothing but heartache.

Her cap and gown were delivered to her that morning.

Too late, Karen thought when she saw them.

In the way that counted most, she had already graduated.

10

It was not as though they didn't go out again. As Karen had anticipated, within twenty-four hours the brunt of Tim's anger had spent itself, and though she knew in her heart that their relationship had been subtly yet permanently altered, they clung to the formalities. There were events in May that could not be ignored.

First among these, of course, was the Prom. They doubled with Gary and Lisa. Tim, who was to emcee the floor show, hired a dinner jacket for the occasion, and Karen wore her first formal, a full-length dress of ivory lace with a tight-fitting bodice and swirling skirt.

Her corsage was an arrangement of pink carnations which caused her mother to gasp with pleasure.

'I wore carnations to my own senior dance,' Mrs Connors said as she fastened the flowers to the shoulder of Karen's dress. 'The gowns were all strapless then, and the girls wore wrist corsages. Three different boys invited me. One was the captain of the football team.'

They had a table to the right of the bandstand, and people kept coming over all during the evening to compliment Lisa and Karen on the decorations. The weeks of cutting and gluing and painting had not been wasted, for the gym had been magically transformed into a springtime garden. Streamers dipped from the ceiling like disoriented rainbows, and bowers of paper blossoms nestled in corners. The walls were covered over with murals depicting rolling hillsides, and the band members wore garlands on their heads and played beneath a canopy of plastic roses.

Senior Notables were announced during intermission, and Karen was more relieved than disappointed to hear two other names called for the 'Cutest Couple' award. Tim was runner-up for 'Best Looking' and received a plaque with a mirror in its centre.

There was no time during the evening in which they were alone together. Because it was the custom for Prom Night festivities to last until dawn, they continued on after the dance to a private party given by a girlfriend of Lisa's. From there they went to the Senior Breakfast at the Pancake House and yawned their way through heaped plates of blueberry waffles, which they washed down with as much coffee as they could stomach.

When they said, 'Goodnight,' at last, it was really 'Good morning.' Through the open toes of her sandals, Karen could feel the damp of dew-laden grass, and the sky in the east was streaked with crimson.

'Thanks. It was fun,' Tim said. 'A really great night.'

'Yes, it was. One I'll always remember.'

They smiled at each other self-consciously. Tim's eyes were puffy from lack of sleep. His tie had twisted to one side, and there was a punch stain on the front of the rented jacket.

'Congratulations,' Karen said, 'for making Notable.'

'*Almost* making it. I'm runner-up, remember?'

'But you got a plaque.'

'Well, sure, and I'm glad it has a mirror. I can hang it in the bathroom and use it to shave by.'

He hesitated for an indiscernible instant and then bent to kiss her. His breath was sour from too much coffee, and both of their mouths were sticky with blueberry syrup.

Out in the street, Gary gave the horn of his car an impatient beep.

'Well, I guess they want to get going,' Tim said awkwardly. 'Have a good sleep. I'll see you at school on Monday.'

'Yes – see you on Monday,' Karen echoed.

The porch light glowed wanly in the grey light of dawn,

and the house seemed strangely silent without the sound of television that usually greeted her.

Feeling almost as though she were an intruder in someone else's home, Karen let herself in, relocked the door, and turned off the outside light. She ascended the stairs, moving as quietly as possible so as not to wake her parents, and went down the hall to her bedroom.

Tossing her evening bag on to the bed, she crossed to the window. The streaks of crimson had grown brighter now, igniting the cloudbank above them, but the globe that was the sun itself remained hidden behind the trees and houses that obscured the horizon.

A poem by Emily Dickinson sprang to her mind:

> *I'll tell you how the sun rose—*
> *A ribbon at a time—*

Would there be a question about that verse in the American Lit. exam? It was certainly possible – but then, as Tim had pointed out, the Lit. test might cover any number of subjects. What they were, she would find out on exam day. If it was, indeed, possible for her to make this discovery before the rest of the class, Karen didn't want to know about it.

Pulling down the blind to shut out the sunlight, she took off her dress and hung it carefully in the closet. The wilted corsage drooped dismally from the shoulder strap, its blossoms already beginning to brown at the edges. During the hours she had worn it, its spicy smell had turned thick and cloying.

Karen climbed into bed and slept dreamlessly until lunchtime.

As it turned out, the focus of the Lit. exam was not on Dickinson at all, but on T. S. Eliot, and the only quote that Mrs Ellsworth asked for was from 'The Hollow Men':

> *This is the way the world ends*
> *Not with a bang but a whimper.*

This is the way that love ends, Karen paraphrased silently, as she sat staring down at the paper. *With a half-hearted kiss on the doorstep and 'See you on Monday.'* Of course, she didn't write that down on the answer sheet.

She made an A on the test, and Tim made a C.

Graduation exercises took place in the gymnasium. The murals were gone from the walls now, and the only indication that a dance had recently been held there was the presence of a tattered strand of crepe paper that had once been part of a streamer and had become snagged on one of the basketball hoops.

As had been previously arranged, Tim and Karen marched down the aisle together, he in a purple gown, she in a white one, with unbecoming squares of cloth-covered cardboard centred on their heads and gold tassels dangling in their faces. After they received their diplomas, they dutifully flicked the tassels to the far side of the caps and joined their classmates in singing the Alma Mater.

It's almost over, Karen kept thinking. It's almost done.

Four years of high school, three of middle school, five of elementary; one year of kindergarten, another of nursery, all had been aimed at bringing her to this one triumphant moment.

Why don't I feel excited? she asked herself without really caring. Why does this seem more like an ending than a beginning?

Her cap had slipped forward and was threatening to slide down over her left eye. She reached up surreptitiously and adjusted it. She glanced sideways at Tim, but he was gazing out across the sea of upturned faces, oblivious to her presence, singing lustily. His own cap was sitting exactly where it should sit, wedged down firmly on his head. His hair came springing out from under its edge in a fringe of dark curls.

Karen tried to recall what that hair had felt like beneath her fingers and was amazed to discover that she could not remember. Only weeks had passed, and she had disposed of the memory already. She had managed to block it out in the same way that she had other painful recollections – the image of a pair of sandals on a pebbled beach – a red bicycle propped against a cottonwood – the smell of slick wet rocks and fast-running river water.

I won't let it hurt me, she told herself. *I will not let it matter.* Her relationship with Tim, as it had once been, was part of another lifetime.

A burst of applause snapped her attention back to the immediate. The rendition of the Alma Mater had been completed, and graduation exercises were over. People were jumping up from their seats now – fathers and mothers, grandparents, brothers and sisters. Tim was gone without a word, swept away into the churning chaos. Karen caught sight of him a few minutes later, standing in the far aisle, being hugged by his mother.

Gazing out across the milling crowd, she saw her own parents. Her father, older and more distinguished looking than most of the other parents, was dressed in the same business suit he had worn to the office that morning. Her mother was wearing a tailored blue dress that Karen had not seen before. They were trying to shove their way towards the front of the gym. Her father was greeted by someone he knew and stopped to exchange pleasantries, but her mother refused to be distracted. She kept ploughing determinedly onward until she reached the aisle that ran parallel to the stage and began to work her way along it, pushing people gently but firmly out of her path.

She reached the stairs and had already started up them when Karen intercepted her.

'Mom – hey – you're not supposed to come up here!'

'Well, you weren't coming *down*,' her mother said accusingly. She put her arms around Karen and hugged her. 'I can't believe it! My baby is all grown up!'

Karen forced a smile. 'I don't *feel* grown up. The truth is, I don't feel much different from the way I felt yesterday.'

'But you *are* different! You're a graduate now. You're at such a wonderful point in life! Everything lies ahead for you! Everything is possible!'

Her mother's arms were thin and strong like bands of steel wire. They tightened convulsively, and for a moment Karen experienced the fleeting thought that she might be sliced in two.

'Oh, to be eighteen again!' Mrs Connors continued. 'Won't you and Tim have fun at the University!'

'College still seems far away,' Karen said evasively. 'There's the whole long summer between now and then.'

'Only three short months, and those will pass quickly. There are such a lot of things we're going to need to do to get you ready. You'll have to have a new wardrobe, for one thing. Girls dress differently in college from the way they do in high school. That lace dress was lovely for the Prom, but it won't be right for sorority parties.'

'There's Dad!' Karen announced, relieved at finding an excuse to steer the conversation away from the subject of dating. 'I don't think he sees us. Wait – yes, he does! He's waving!'

'I thought we'd lost him for good,' Mrs Connors said testily. 'That man can't go anywhere without finding somebody to talk business with.'

As her mother's arms released her, Karen moved gratefully into her father's less frenetic embrace.

'Congratulations!' he said, thrusting her out at arm's length to get a better look at her. 'My daughter, the sweet girl graduate! We need to get a picture!'

'I told you to bring the camera,' his wife interjected. 'If you'd ever pay any attention—'

'I meant to bring it,' said Mr Connors. 'I had it all set out and everything, and then, just as we were getting ready to leave, I had a phone call. By the time I could get done with that we were so rushed that I ended up going off and leaving the camera on the table in the den.'

'You can take the picture when we get back to the house,' Karen told him. 'We don't need the gym for background.'

'There'll be time enough for that tomorrow,' said her mother. 'You don't have to come straight back home with us, Karen. There have to be celebration events that you and Tim want to be part of. This is a special evening for the two of you.'

'Not really,' said Karen. 'I mean, there aren't any parties I want to go to.'

'Now, don't try to tell me that. This is your graduation night!'

'Mom, I'm grown now, right? You just said it yourself,' Karen said. 'I should know if I want to go to any parties. If I say I don't want to, then I don't *want* to.'

'But, what about Tim?' Mrs Connors asked her. 'Surely, he must be planning—'

'Tim can take care of himself,' said Karen. 'If Tim had wanted to take me to a party, he would have invited me. As it happens, he didn't.'

'But, I thought—' Her mother paused, digesting Karen's statement. She seemed to reconsider what she had been about to say and stop herself. 'I see. I didn't realise that you were having problems.'

'We're not *having* them,' Karen said. 'We've *had* them. It's over between Tim and me.'

'But he took you to the Prom! And tonight you walked together!'

'We signed up to be graduation partners back in April,' Karen told her. 'That was a preset thing. There's no rule that says that if you walk with a partner you have to go out together afterwards.'

'Parties are group affairs,' Mrs Connors said. 'Your other friends will be attending them. I'm sure you'd be as welcome without a date as you would be with one.'

'I told you, I'm not interested in going,' said Karen.

'There's no reason, then, that you have to,' said her father. 'Lovers' quarrels tend to work themselves out, though, daughter. Things will look brighter in the morning.'

'You're probably right,' said Karen, avoiding her mother's eyes. There were questions that she did not want to have to answer.

The parking lot was jammed with more cars than it would have held if it had been a school day. There were people everywhere – graduates still in their caps and gowns, graduates changed into street clothes, friends and relatives hugging and laughing – all of them in a state of exultation. The continual flashes of light that spattered the darkness proved that there were many who had not forgotten their cameras.

Because they had arrived late, Karen's parents had been forced to park at the back of the lot next to the athletic field. Now, it took over ten minutes to work their way into the line of cars that were inching towards the street. Traffic from both sides of the lot merged at the exit gate, and the car that pulled into line directly ahead of them was a familiar Pontiac filled with teenagers. Karen could not see into the front seat to identify the driver, but when one of the girls in the back turned to make a laughing remark to the boy beside her, she recognised the profile of Lisa Honeycutt.

So Tim was attending the graduation parties without her. Karen accepted the knowledge without real surprise. Although it was impossible to see whether or not he had a date sitting next to him, the mere fact that he was providing transportation for so many people showed that his plans for the evening had not been made on impulse.

These were classmates whom Karen had begun to think

of as her friends as well as Tim's. It was painful to realise that she had been mistaken. It was doubtful, she knew, that she was being deliberately excluded and someone had actually suggested, 'Let's go off and leave Karen.' Still, not one of the group had cared enough to insist that she be with them. She had been accepted as part of a unit – 'Tim-and-Karen' – and if that unit no longer existed, then Karen didn't either.

I will *not* feel hurt, she told herself. It just doesn't matter. I'm no worse off now than I was before Tim and I started dating. For a while things changed, and now they're back to the way they used to be; that's all.

Her parents did not seem to have recognised Tim's car, or, if they had, they restrained themselves from commenting. The conversation during the drive home was confined solely to the topic of the graduation exercises.

When they reached the house, Karen's father retrieved his camera from the table in the den and set out to make up for his earlier forgetfulness by turning the photography session into a professional-style undertaking. First he took formal close-ups, using the white drapes in the living room for a backdrop; then he shot a batch of full-length poses of Karen standing on the stairs, holding her diploma.

After those had been taken, he turned to his wife.

'Why don't you go stand on the step beside her? I'll get a shot of the two of you together.'

'Oh, no,' Mrs Connors objected. 'This is supposed to be *Karen's* night.'

'Sure, it is, but you're her mother. It's your graduation too. You've invested eighteen years in this young woman.'

'Come on, Mum,' Karen said dutifully. 'We haven't had a picture taken together since I was a baby.'

'Well – if you really want me to.' Her mother sounded pleased.

She ascended the stairs and took her place next to her

daughter. They stood there stiffly, shoulder to shoulder, directing their smiles towards the camera lens.

The flash exploded in their faces.

'Is that it, then?' asked Karen, relieved to have the ordeal over with. 'If it is, I'm going to get changed. This outfit is sweltering.'

'It's not as bad as what I had to wear at *my* graduation,' said her mother. 'My gown was made of wool, and it gave me a rash, but at the party afterwards I wore a red silk dress.' She reached over suddenly and placed her hand upon Karen's. 'It's all been worth it.'

'What has?' asked Karen. 'Renting the gown?'

'Having a child. Devoting my life to raising and protecting her. Seeing you up there on that stage tonight, standing so straight, looking so beautiful, so much a real *part* of it all, I felt very proud.'

'Why, Mom!' Karen exclaimed, surprised and touched.

The flash went off again, momentarily blinding them.

Startled, Karen swung back around to confront her father.

'I thought the picture taking was supposed to be over!'

'I had one shot left on the roll,' Mr Connors told her. 'I wanted to use it up. I'm finished now. You can go change your clothes if you want to.'

'I do want to,' said Karen. 'Actually, I guess I'll say goodnight. I'm tired out from all the excitement. I think I'll take a shower and read in bed.'

'On your graduation night!' her mother exclaimed incredulously. 'Honestly, there are times when I just don't understand you, Karen. I was sure that once you had a chance to think things over, you'd change your mind about going out with your friends. You could take the car and be on your own, you know. You wouldn't have to be dependent on Tim for anything.'

Karen sighed. Her mother was back in character. The

surge of affection that she had felt for her only moments before was replaced by exasperation.

'I haven't changed my mind,' she said. 'I don't want to go out. Why does that bother you so much?'

'I didn't say it bothered me,' her mother said. 'I don't appreciate it when you use that tone of voice. You make it sound as though I were out to wreck your life. You know perfectly well that all I want is for you to have a good time.'

'I do know that,' Karen admitted. 'It's just that, sometimes—' She couldn't think how to complete the sentence without antagonising her mother further.

Her father came to her rescue.

'How about some television?' he suggested. 'Isn't it just about time for "Saturday Night Live"?'

That night, Karen dreamed. This had not occurred for so many weeks now that she had begun to dare to hope that this phase of her life was over.

This dream, like the earlier ones, was about a child. This time, however, the subject was one she had never seen. She was small and blonde, and she stood next to a backyard swing set. Beyond that, there was a wooden fence that was bordered by a line of rose bushes. The bushes were in bloom, spilling forth great clusters of pink and yellow blossoms. The little girl stood facing them. All that Karen could see of her was her back and a pale, silken torrent of hair.

The sight of the child stirred an emotion in her that was more intense than anything she had ever experienced. It was a surge of caring so overpowering that it was as though a steel blade were being twisted in her heart.

Who are you? Karen called out to the dream-child. *Please, turn around so I can see you! I want to know you! I want to see your face!*

But the girl did not hear. She was busy with the roses.

Turn around, Karen begged her.

A surge of fear shot through her, for abruptly she knew

that this child was in danger. How the knowledge came to her, she could not have said, but she was as certain of its validity as she had been of the fate of Carla Sanchez.

Be careful! Karen cried silently.

The little girl bent and kissed a rosebud.

Karen awakened, shaking and drenched in sweat.

11

In the clear light of morning, she was able to put the dream into perspective.

'It was a nightmare,' she assured herself. 'Just a regular nightmare, like anybody in the world could have. Every dream I have doesn't have to be prophetic. I was hurt and mad about Tim, and, because I wouldn't admit it, my feelings showed up in my dreaming.'

The explanation was reasonable, especially in light of the fact that the child in the dream had been fey and featureless, as compared with the images of Carla and of Bobby Zenner, which had seemed concrete enough to touch.

It was just a dream. It didn't have any deeper meaning.

Eager as she was to believe this, Karen, nevertheless, forced herself to leaf carefully through the morning paper, flipping the pages apprehensively, alert for news of some small blonde girl whose family might have reported her missing. There was no such story, nor was there any such report on television.

Three days later, having shoved the dream firmly to the back of her mind, Karen started her job at the Heights Day Care Centre.

'Are you sure that's what you want to do?' her mother asked doubtfully. 'You've worked at that place for two whole summers. It was a good enough job when you were in high school, but now that you've graduated, I should think you'd want to look for something more stimulating.'

'I'll keep my eyes open,' Karen assured her. 'If something irresistible comes along, I can always make a job switch.'

She had made a conscious decision to avoid argument with her mother. It had become obvious on the night of her graduation that the two of them had reached a point at which they could not continue to live together. In

September, Karen would be moving into a college dormitory, which would provide them with an automatic separation point. Next summer, if things went as she anticipated, she would find a job, perhaps in another town, that would pay enough so that she could afford her own apartment.

Meanwhile, she would try to avoid confrontations. Since this would probably be the last occasion on which they would be living in the same home, she hoped that she and her mother could manage to get through it with a minimum amount of conflict.

Despite this resolution, she had no intention of sacrificing her final summer at the Centre, no matter what other jobs might present themselves. She loved the Centre and everyone connected with it—Mrs Dunn, the director; plump, efficient Jane Roebuck, who taught the four- and five-year-olds; pretty, round-faced Maria Torres, who cared for the infants. Most of all, she loved the atmosphere: the warmth and good spirits that pervaded the clean, airy rooms, the clatter and clutter and whimpers and giggles, the shouts on the playground, the chortles and squeals and cooing in the Baby Room.

'Am I ever glad to see *you*!' Mrs Dunn, silver-haired and bustling, greeted Karen with unconcealed relief when she reported to work the Monday after graduation. 'Things are absolutely chaotic around here! We lost our playground help – both girls fell through on us without a word of warning – and you did know, didn't you, that Maria got married?'

'No!' exclaimed Karen. 'I didn't even know she was engaged!'

'She wasn't. That is, not officially. It was one of those love-at-first-sight things, a wild, romantic elopement. Which was lovely for Maria, but devastating for us. I've hired one new girl, and I'm looking for two others, and I've been living in terror that you might change your mind about coming back this year.'

'No way,' Karen told her. 'You can stop worrying. You can count on the fact that I'm not running off to get married.'

'Thank God for small favours,' said Mrs Dunn. 'What I was hoping was that you would take over the Baby Room. That would leave me free to take the toddlers, and poor Jane will just have to manage as best she can with the preschoolers until I can hire some extra help.'

'How many babies do we have this year?' Karen asked her.

'Eight to ten regulars, which is too many, I know, but you'll have Deedee, our new girl, to help you. She's only fifteen, but she has little brothers. That should make her an expert at diaper changing.'

'That's great,' said Karen. 'You know how much I like the babies.'

The previous year, she had been Maria's assistant in the Baby Room, so, this year, as she entered the familiar environment, it was with the happy feeling that she was coming home. The cribs and infant seats were not yet occupied, but the room itself held the sweet, residual odour of Pampers and talcum powder. A pile of towels and crib sheets, fresh from the laundry, sat out on the changing table. Coloured mobiles swirled lazily in a current of air from an open window, and the yellow walls and bright, checkered curtains threw off a glow like reflected sunlight.

Deedee proved to be a skinny, freckled girl who announced a bit sullenly that this was her first job and that she had applied for it under duress.

'My mother said she didn't want me sitting around all summer,' she grumbled. 'I don't see why that would have been so terrible. After beating my brains out at school all year, I deserve a vacation.'

'You'll have fun working here,' Karen assured her. 'I started two summers ago at almost the same age as you are, and I liked it so well I've come back every year.'

Their conversation was interrupted by the tinkle of the handbell in the front office, announcing the beginning of the first rush hour of the day.

The Centre opened its doors at seven on weekday mornings, and working-mother clients began bringing in children almost immediately. By seven fifteen on this particular day, a line of parents stood in wait at the admissions desk, and eight small inhabitants had already been installed in the Baby Room. Two of these were too young to do anything much but sleep. The other six, who were in various stages of mobility, had been placed in playpens and bounce chairs and were busily engaged in gumming graham crackers.

Shortly before nine, an attractive young woman rushed in with a ten-month-old named Matthew, announcing frantically that she was late for class. Several other college-bound parents, all equally harried, arrived just behind her. There was then a lull until midmorning, at which time there was a rash of new arrivals brought in by mothers who were headed for luncheons or club activities.

For identification purposes, the names of the babies were printed on cards and pinned to their shirt fronts.

'Adam – Sara – Matthew – another Adam.' Deedee reviewed them aloud. 'They all of them sound as though they come straight from the Bible.'

'This is the year for that,' said Mrs Dunn, who had stuck her head in through the doorway to review the situation. 'The names seem to come in batches. Last season's babies were Heathers and Brookes and Skyes.'

She glanced worriedly around the room, which was churning like an anthill.

'You're over your quota here, aren't you? I've put out a sign, saying that we're filled, which is something I should have done a half hour ago. It's time for me to take the toddlers out to the playground. Are the two of you going to be able to handle things here?'

'We're doing all right,' Karen said. 'The problem will come at lunchtime.'

'It will be hectic, for sure,' Mrs Dunn agreed. 'I'm sorry to have swamped you like this. Darn that Maria! Why couldn't she have picked a more convenient time to find her Prince Charming!'

Serving lunch in the Baby Room made the remembered task of feeding one lone Stephanie Zenner seem like nothing. Even back when Maria had been there to supervise, lunch hour had been known to stretch from late morning until early afternoon. Food had to be spooned in turn into first one gaping mouth and then another, while the children who were old enough to feed themselves splashed and splattered and dumped their least favourite items off their trays. Slumbering infants woke and cried and were changed and given bottles, and older babies went down for or got up from naps, overlapping each other's sleep schedules in rapid succession.

'What a madhouse!' gasped Deedee. 'And I thought that feeding twin brothers was bad!'

'You'll get used to it,' said Karen.

'Not if I can help it, I won't.' She was attempting to administer a bottle with one hand and screw the top off a jar of apple sauce with the other. 'How can you keep coming back here summer after summer?'

'I enjoy it,' Karen told her. 'I can't explain it. It just feels like the right place for me to be.'

At midafternoon things suddenly became more peaceful. By now, several mothers had returned to pick up their children, and many of the remaining infants were sleeping. The others were resting quietly in their cribs, content for the moment to allow themselves to be hypnotised by the motion of the dangling mobiles and the shifting pattern of shadows they created on the wall behind them.

With a sigh of exaggerated exhaustion, Deedee collapsed into a chair.

'I'm dead,' she moaned. 'I may never get up again. And to make things worse, you guys don't even own a Coke machine. How can a person keep up her energy?'

'There's a chemist across the street,' said Karen. 'Since things have quieted down, I guess you could go—'

As if on cue, one of the babies gave a demanding grunt and began to haul himself to a standing position in his crib.

'Oh, no!' exclaimed Deedee. 'Now that one's going to wake up all the rest of them! Doesn't it ever stop? I'm getting ready for a nervous breakdown!'

'You sit there and rest,' Karen told her. 'I don't seem to be as tired as you are.'

She crossed to the struggling youngster, who was straining and puffing like a mountain climber attempting to scale Mount Everest.

'Hello there, Matthew,' she said, impressed by his perseverance. 'You're not much of a sleeper, are you?'

The child paused at half-mast, knees bent, hands gripping the railing, and regarded her thoughtfully with brilliant blue eyes. Then, as though it had suddenly occurred to him that this unfamiliar person might be in a position to release him from his confinement, he broke into an ingratiating grin, displaying a set of four tiny white teeth.

'Boy, are you a charmer!' exclaimed Karen, reaching into the crib to hoist him to her shoulder. 'With that smile and those eyes, your folks ought to rent you out as a model.'

'No way,' said Deedee. 'He'd never sit still long enough to pose.'

'Well, maybe he could make it in television. Would you like that, Matthew? Would it be fun to be in a Gerber's commercial?'

Karen hugged the little boy against her, enjoying the sweet smell of his downy skin and the feathery touch of the soft hair. Until this moment, she had not fully realised how much she missed cuddling a baby.

The Zenners had broken contact with her completely.

She understood why, of course, and she couldn't blame them. She was not the only person who must suffer from nightmares. The vision of their son, unconscious in a car trunk, would remain with Bobby's parents as long as it would with her.

Matthew took hold of a lock of her hair and yanked it. 'Ow!' Karen exclaimed in mock agony. 'Please, Matthew, don't pull my hair out!'

The baby giggled and made a grab for her left ear. He gave it an experimental tug and paused expectantly.

Extending the game, Karen said 'Ow!' again and shook her head fiercely. The plump little hand gripped her harder, and she was rewarded this time by a whole torrent of mischievous giggles.

'It looks as though Matt-the-Monster has found a new victim!'

The voice spoke unexpectedly from behind her.

Karen turned to find the slender, strikingly pretty girl who had brought Matthew to the Centre that morning observing them with amusement from the doorway to the kitchen.

'I'm Sue Wilson, Matt's battered mother,' she continued. 'I couldn't park in front because of the laundry truck, so I left the car in the alley and came in through the back.'

The moment he heard his mother's voice, Matthew had begun to squirm in Karen's arms. Now he let out an impatient squeal and lunged forward with so much vigour that it was all she could do to keep from dropping him.

'Hi, Matt! Come and see Mommy!' Sue Wilson held out her arms for her son. 'The truth is, it's amazing the poor kid knows who I am, we get so little time together. My days are spent in class, and evenings I'm at the law library.'

'You're in law school?' Karen was unable to hide her surprise. The girl's features and figure seemed more in keeping with the image of a fashion model.

'I was a first-year law student when Steve and I married.

Then – surprise! – along came Matt, and I had to drop out for a semester. Now, I'm back again and wondering if it's worth it. The career, I mean, not the baby. Or maybe I do mean the baby. Actually, I guess I don't know *what* I mean.' The girl gave a short, apologetic laugh. 'You'll have to forgive me. I've been studying for finals, and I'm reeling.'

'I know the feeling,' said Deedee. 'No one who goes to school fulltime should have to do anything else, even in the summers.'

'Matt's a hunk,' said Karen. 'Those incredible eyes!'

'They run in his father's family,' Matthew's mother told her. 'My husband and brother-in-law both have them, and so does Matt's grandmother. It's odd, because the genes for dark eyes are supposed to take precedence over light ones, but in their family blue eyes are a dominant trait.'

Karen said, 'Despite problems, I know you must be glad you have Matt.'

'We adore him, of course,' Sue Wilson said defensively. 'It would have been easier, though, if he'd come along a few years later.' As if to soften the impact of her words, she gave the baby a hug and swung him around so that he was straddling one of her narrow hips. 'Well, we're off to buy groceries, and then to the laundromat, and then home to fix dinner. Does that laundry service you use do private deliveries, or is that just for businesses?'

'They deliver to anybody,' Karen told her. 'You have to pay extra, though.'

She was so irritated by the woman's attitude towards motherhood that it did not occur to her, at that moment, to analyse the content of their conversation. Later, when she thought back upon it, she would realise that there had been no reason for a laundry truck to have been parked in front of the Centre. The clean sheets and towels had been delivered only that morning.

12

On Thursday, it rained. It didn't start out as a heavy rain, and Karen awoke to the smell of it rather than the sound. She lay in bed with her eyes still closed, breathing in the dampness, and knew without looking that the sky outside the window was thick and low and that the leaves of the backyard elm were glistening with drops of silver.

It was one of those on-again-off-again, all-day drizzles, the kind that keep you disconcerted. When she left the house to walk to the bus stop, it had let up completely, and she almost didn't bother to take a rain scarf. Then, at the last moment, she did tuck one into her purse, and she was later glad that she had, for by the time the bus pulled to a stop at the corner of Central Avenue and Hill Street, the softly glowing, mother-of-pearl day had dulled and darkened, and rain had begun to fall again.

Huddled close to the side of a building under the protection of an overhang, Karen tied the scarf over her hair, irritated at herself for not having had the good sense to ask her mother to drive her. To reduce the friction between them, she had been trying lately to make as few demands as possible, particularly in connection with her job. The Centre opened so early that Mrs Connors was usually still sleeping when Karen left in the morning, and to wake her with a request for transportation had promised to produce more problems than it would solve. She hadn't realised that the rain would pick up again so quickly. Now that it had, the idea of a six-block hike through a steady downpour was not at all enticing.

She was in the process of reminding herself that she wasn't going to melt like the Wicked Witch of the West just because some water fell on her, when a car with a

Texas licence plate pulled to a halt in the lane across from her.

The woman who was driving leaned across the front seat and rolled down the window on the passenger's side.

'Excuse me,' she called. 'Do you know the way to the Heights Day Care Centre?'

'Yes,' Karen told her. 'In fact, I work there. You're on the right street, but you're headed in the wrong direction.'

'You mean, I've already passed it? I didn't see a sign out front.' The woman sounded exasperated. 'Are you headed there now? If so, hop in, and I'll drive you. I will, that is, if you can give me directions so I can find the place.'

'That would be wonderful,' Karen said gratefully. 'I wasn't looking forward to a six-block swim upstream.'

She hurried across the street, dodging puddles and ducking her head to prevent the rain from pelting her face. As she opened the car door, she peered automatically into the back, expecting to see a car bed and a diaper bag.

To her surprise, the seat was empty.

The woman caught her glance and interpreted it correctly.

'I'm not looking for child care. I have an appointment for a job interview. The girl I talked with on the phone said the Centre was hiring new staff.' She waited until Karen had pulled the door closed and then pushed a button to activate the lock. Throwing the car into gear, she pressed her foot down on the accelerator. 'I'm going to be meeting with a Mrs Dunn. She's the director, isn't she?'

'Yes,' said Karen. 'You'll like her. She's a really great person to work for.'

'I hope I have a chance to find that out,' the woman said. 'I'm new here, and I'm discovering that finding a job in an unfamiliar city is as hard as pulling hens' teeth.'

Leaning back in her seat, Karen regarded her companion with casual curiosity. She was an ordinary-looking woman, in her middle to late thirties, with blunt, nondescript features and the sort of milky, lightly freckled skin that usually belongs only to redheads. Her hair, however, had no hint of red in it. It was the same pale shade as Karen's and fell loosely to the shoulders in a style that seemed too young for the face it was framing.

Sensing the friendly inspection, the woman glanced across and smiled.

'Have you worked at the Centre long?' she asked conversationally.

'This is my third summer,' said Karen. 'I went out job hunting the spring I turned sixteen so my parents wouldn't force me to go to tennis camp. The timing was lucky. The girl who helped with the two- and three-year-olds had decided to go to summer school, so Mrs Dunn hired me to take her place. The next year, she made me assistant in the Baby Room, and this year she's put me in charge there.'

' "The Baby Room," ' the woman repeated. 'That's a cute thing to call it. How many infants do you have to take care of?'

'It varies,' Karen told her. 'We've got ten or so regulars, but you can never be sure about the drop-ins. There are some mothers who drop their kids off for just an hour or so every now and then when they want to go shopping or out to lunch or to get their hair done.'

She realised, suddenly, that she had become distracted and had not been paying attention to where they were going.

'I'm sorry,' she said. 'I forgot I was supposed to be giving directions. You'll want to get turned around and headed back north again. The Centre's up Hill Street, a block past the public library.'

'We don't need to worry about that just yet,' her new friend told her. 'First, I'm going to have to make a swing by my apartment.'

Karen regarded her with surprise.

'I thought we were going straight to the Centre.'

'We were,' the woman said. 'That's what I originally intended, that is, but I've suddenly realised that I don't have my résumé with me.' She gave a short, apologetic laugh. 'I feel so foolish. I stayed up half the night writing and typing that thing, and then I must have walked out this morning and left it on the breakfast table.'

'Will this take long?' Karen said apprehensively. 'I was supposed to have been at work ten minutes ago.'

'It will hardly take any time at all,' the woman told her. 'My place isn't far from here. Besides, that clock on the dashboard isn't accurate. I don't think it's even seven yet.' She had turned the car east now, on to a side street. 'Tell me more about the Centre, Karen. Are you in sole charge of the Baby Room? If I do get hired, do you think I'll become your assistant?'

'Probably not,' said Karen. 'There's a girl named Deedee who's working with me already. What's most likely is that you'll be put with Jane Roebuck, who's got the kindergarten kids. She has no one to help her, and she really needs somebody.'

It was a trivial exchange, but something about it disturbed her. Karen shifted uncomfortably in her seat, unable to pinpoint exactly what it was. The woman's question had certainly been reasonable, and the answer had been a simple one to give. Why was it that she had the disconcerting feeling that she had allowed something of real significance to slip past her?

Something had been said that shouldn't have been, something that had caught at the edge of her consciousness but not fully registered.

She let her mind slide back over the woman's side of the conversation.

'. . . I'm going to have to make a swing by my apartment . . . I don't have my résumé . . . I feel so foolish . . . My place isn't far . . . Tell me more about the Centre, Karen. Are you in sole charge of the . . .?'

Something clicked. She ran that sentence through again – 'Tell me more about the Centre, Karen.' That was it! That was the word that shouldn't have been there – it was her own name!

This stranger had called her 'Karen', yet at no time since their meeting had Karen introduced herself other than to volunteer the fact that she was an employee of the Day Care Centre.

Something cold touched her spine – the chilly finger of fear.

None of this is what it seems. This woman knew who I was before she picked me up. She knew that I would be there, on that particular corner, at that particular time.

Karen drew a long slow breath, trying to still the sudden pounding of her heart.

'You haven't told me who *you* are,' she said, struggling to make the statement sound natural. 'You know my name, but I don't know yours.'

'Betty Smith,' the woman said easily.

'That's simple to remember.'

It was almost *too* simple. It was the kind of name that one might snatch at random out of nowhere when asked suddenly to produce one.

The traffic light at the intersection one block ahead of them had just changed from green to yellow. That meant that by the time they reached it, it would be red. Karen's purse lay on her lap, and both her hands had been resting casually on top of it. Now, she lifted her left hand slightly, causing her purse to tilt sideways and block the view of the driver. Surreptitiously, she began to move her right hand along the seat. She kept her eyes carefully focused upon the road.

'It's just a couple of more blocks now,' said Betty Smith. 'If you like, you can give Mrs Dunn a call from my apartment to let her know what's held you up and that you're on your way.'

She was slowing the car in preparation for the stop at the light. With her left hand, Karen tightened her grip on her purse. She did not change the direction of her gaze, for fear of alerting her companion to her intentions, but she did let her right hand drift up from the seat until it hovered opposite the handle of the door.

The light changed to red, and the car rolled to a complete stop.

Karen's hand shot out with the speed of a striking cobra and closed upon the cold metal of the door handle. She gave it a hard thrust downward, at the same time hurling the full weight of her body against the door. She did not worry about trying to retain her balance; with the traffic halted around them, she was prepared to roll straight out on to the street if she had to in order to escape from the car.

Her shoulder struck the door with bruising force, but it did not fly open as she had expected. The handle had not responded to the pressure of her hand.

'What did you want to go and do that for?' Betty Smith asked quietly. 'You could hurt yourself that way. The lock control switch is here on the driver's side. That door isn't going to open unless I press the release button.'

'Then, press it!' Karen demanded. 'I want to get out!'

'You can, very soon now. We're almost to my apartment.'

'I don't want to go to your apartment,' said Karen. 'I want to get out here – right here – at this traffic light!'

'I'm afraid that won't be possible,' her companion told her.

The light had clicked to green now, and the car was again in motion.

The chill that Karen had experienced a few moments earlier had by this time spread throughout her entire body. She could feel it from her scalp to the soles of her feet.

It took effort to keep her voice steady.

'How did you know what my name was? I never told you.'

There was a slight pause.

Then Betty Smith said, 'That wasn't difficult. All I had to do was phone the Centre and ask them.'

'Ask them – *what?*'

'I said that I was a working mother in search of day care for my three-month-old daughter, and I asked who the person was who would be taking care of her if I brought her to the Centre. They said it would be Karen Connors. I asked if that was the older woman with the grey hair, and they said, no, that Karen was young and blonde.'

'Then, all the things you told me before were lies!' Karen exclaimed incredulously. 'You don't really have a job interview lined up today! You didn't forget any résumé! You never had any intention of driving me to the Centre!'

'That's true,' the woman said without apology.

'You must be crazy!' said Karen. 'Why would you want to go to so much trouble just to find out who was in charge of the Baby Room? Why did you pick me up this morning? What are you planning to do?'

'You'll know soon enough,' Betty Smith told her. 'Here we are at last. Behold to the right – the exotic Tumbleweed Apartments!'

Karen turned to stare through the side window at the long row of brown stucco buildings. In front of one of these there stood a crudely printed sign, reading 'Vacancies – Best Rates in Town – Apply Within'. Dull, peeling paint that might once have been bright turquoise hung in weathered strips from the wooden roof trim and from the frames of the windows. There was no landscaping, though the small patches of dirt that served as front yards separating the line of faded blue doors from the street were dotted occasionally with tufts of dry, unwatered grass.

'They're not exactly luxurious,' the woman said lightly. 'They do have their advantages, though. The neighbours aren't snoopy, and neither is the manager. If you pay rent in advance, you can expect to go indefinitely without being bothered by anybody.'

She continued to drive on past the line of buildings to the end of the block, where she turned right on to a side street, and then immediately right again, in order to enter an alley behind the apartment complex.

A delivery van with the name 'Sanicare Laundry' lettered on its side was parked some fifty yards up the block. Betty Smith pulled up behind it and stopped the car.

Before she had even had time to switch off the ignition, the door of the van swung open and a stocky, bearded man climbed out of it. He glanced quickly up and down the alley, and then, apparently satisfied that they were its only occupants, came swiftly over to the car.

Betty pressed the button by the steering wheel that released the locks. The man pulled the door open, reached in, and seized Karen's arm.

'Come on,' he said. 'Get out.'

'Let go of me,' Karen said shakily. 'I'm not going anywhere with you.'

'I said get out!' the man repeated. 'Move it! We don't have all day!'

His strong, stubby fingers bit cruelly into the soft flesh of her upper arm.

'Let me alone!' cried Karen. 'Stop it! You're hurting me!'

In a desperate attempt to break his grip, she swung around to face him, clawing at his fingers with her free left hand and kicking out frantically with her feet. As she struggled, she drew in her breath in preparation to scream.

Before she could get the sound out of her throat, however, her assailant realised her intention and clamped his other hand across her mouth with so much force that her upper teeth sliced into her lip. Stunned by the shock of pain, and gagging on the sudden rush of blood that filled her mouth, Karen found herself being hauled bodily out of her seat. An instant later, she was being propelled through the open back door and into the kitchen of one of the apartments.

Betty seemed to materialise out of nowhere. Following them in, she threw the door closed and locked it, and then leaned back against it, breathing hard.

The jarring slam was followed by a long, strange moment of silence.

The man was the first to recover himself.

'The girl's a damned wildcat!'

'Surprise, surprise!' Betty seemed amused by his statement. 'She doesn't look much like one, does she? Appearances can deceive you. Do you know she even tried to jump out of the car while I was driving?'

'Great,' the man said sarcastically. 'That would have been just great. People screaming, police cars, ambulances – what a show!'

'Come off it, Jed,' said Betty. 'There was no danger of that; I had the doors locked. Tie our little friend up, and let's get going. You did get gas, didn't you, and the road map?'

'You don't have to worry about things on my end,' the man told her. 'You just concentrate on taking care of your own job. It's time to make that phone call. We don't want the director calling the girl's home to check on why she hasn't come in yet.'

'That's what I'm getting ready to do right now,' said Betty. 'The minute I'm off that phone, though, I want us out of here.'

All during the time that they had been talking, the man's hand had been pressed down firmly upon Karen's mouth. Now, he removed it, grimacing in disgust when he found that his palm was sticky with blood.

'Lie down,' he ordered.

'No,' Karen told him. She winced with the painful effort of forming the word with her injured lips.

'That's up to you, baby. Stand up, if you want; I couldn't care less. I'll tell you one thing, though; you give me a hard time, and you're going to lose those pretty white teeth. The mouth they come out of won't be in such good shape, either.'

They had things well organised. A ball of twine, a pair of scissors and a dish towel had been laid out in advance on the kitchen table. The man jerked the rain scarf off Karen's head and tossed it on to the stove top. Then he took the towel and tied it tightly across her mouth, knotting it firmly behind her head.

While he was securing her wrists and ankles, Karen could hear Betty's voice chattering away on the telephone in the adjoining room.

'This is Mrs Connors, Karen's mother,' she was saying in the easy, conversational tone that she seemed able to manufacture with so much facility. 'Karen's down with some sort of flu bug. She's running a fever. She's terribly upset about having to leave you in the lurch today, but there's just no way—'

There was a pause.

'Of course, she can't help it,' Betty continued with a little laugh. 'I keep trying to tell her that, but you know Karen – she's worried to death because you're understaffed. My younger sister – I'm sure Karen's mentioned her Aunt Nancy, hasn't she? – has offered to substitute for her. Nancy loves children; she has two of her own, and she's especially marvellous with little babies.'

There was another pause, a shorter one this time.

'Oh, but she wants to!' Betty said. 'She really does! She and Karen are more like good friends than like aunt and niece . . . Yes, really. She's happy to help . . . Oh, great – that's wonderful! Karen will be so relieved . . . Yes, I will. I'll certainly tell her that. Goodbye.'

There was the sharp, clicking sound of the receiver being placed back on the hook.

A moment later, Betty appeared in the kitchen doorway. She was smiling.

'Mrs Dunn sends her love,' she said pleasantly to Karen. 'She says to tell you to get lots of rest and get well fast.'

'That might be easier if she stays off her feet for a while,' the man said cryptically.

He bent quickly and took hold of Karen's ankles. With one hard jerk, he yanked them out from under her.

She fell amazingly slowly, or so it seemed. As if suspended in space, Karen witnessed in slow motion the corner of the stove rising in a graceful, swooping arc to make contact with her forehead. She saw the grease spattered linoleum that lay beyond it and knew that, if she survived the blow that was to come, this patch of floor was the spot on which she would next know consciousness.

There was time, an unbelievable amount of time, in which to comprehend it all. There was time to think of the Day Care Centre – of dear, trusting Mrs Dunn with her arms stretched wide in gratitude to welcome Karen's Aunt Nancy-Betty into the fold. To think of her mother – but, why of her? That was surprising, yet there she was, stopped short in the middle of folding laundry. In her hands she gripped the corners of a bedsheet. Her eyes were wide and startled, and her face was contorted as though in sudden fear.

Karen fell slowly, so slowly that there was time for everything.

There was even time for her to envision in that one final instant before her head struck hard metal, the flickering image of a small blonde child.

13

The awareness of the pain came as slowly as the fall itself. At first it was dull and far, like a memory of something that had not really occurred. Numbed and safe in her padded prison of semiconsciousness, Karen heard the sound of it humming away in the distance like some great drugged bumblebee, unable to find its way out of the thickets and into the garden of her mind.

Lying motionless with her eyes squeezed closed, she waited for the inevitable moment at which sensation would come flooding in. The buzzing drew nearer, and the pain sharpened and began to find its focus in her left temple. Somewhere in her mind's garden, a child was playing – the airy, spindrift, butterfly child whom she had met in dreams.

I must protect her! Karen told herself. *I must keep the bee away!*

She could hear the terrible flapping of the wide, sweeping wings now, as pain came closer, pounding the thick air with a sound like drumrolls. Then it was upon her! It exploded into her consciousness with a stinging siren shriek that seemed to shatter her brain.

She tried to scream, but she couldn't. The unuttered cry backed up in her throat and threatened to strangle her. The pain's force swept her to the brink of consciousness, and she teetered there precariously. Reluctant to face the realities that lay before her, she reached frantically behind her to clutch at the last slim hope of oblivion.

If you don't wake up, the child will die!

There was no one there to have spoken the words, and yet she heard them. If she had not known better, she might even have thought that the voice was her mother's. Whatever its source, she accepted the validity of the statement; if she once gave way to the temptation to slide back into comforting darkness, the little girl would be lost.

That allowed no choice.

With a wrenching effort, Karen forced open her eyes.

She was lying, as she had known she would be, on the floor of the kitchen of one of the Tumbleweed Apartments. Her first impression was of a soot-streaked ceiling swaying uncertainly above her. An unadorned light bulb was suspended at its centre, and beyond that, positioned over the doorway, there was a smoke alarm. The ceiling kept dipping and rippling like a wind-tossed awning, and the bulb lurched drunkenly. The smoke alarm looked like a straining black eye that could not quite seem to get itself into focus.

Karen closed her own eyes and then reopened them, willing the world to stabilise around her. Her head was throbbing with pain. Mercifully, the light in the room was dim; the only source of illumination was a window above the sink, and over that someone had pulled a curtain. The daylight that did seep in was so diffused by the gauzy material that it was difficult to ascertain the colour of the kitchen walls. Eventually, as her eyes became better adjusted, Karen decided that they must be yellow and that the slick, dark areas were grease. The odd-shaped spots that studded the woodwork around the door appeared to be handprints. Because she was lying on her back, she could not see the floor, but from the odour that assaulted her nostrils, there seemed to be little doubt that the apartment's tenants, either current or previous, had owned a cat.

There was no cat here now, and there were no people. The place sang with emptiness. In the world beyond, Karen could hear sounds of activity. A rush of water and the groan of belching pipes proclaimed the fact that someone in an adjoining apartment was taking a shower. Doors were being opened and slammed shut; voices were calling back and forth. She could hear car engines revving up, and in the alley on the far side of the kitchen wall there was the clatter of garbage cans.

It was hard to know for certain how long it had taken her to regain consciousness, but since the complex had not yet settled into mid-morning quiet, Karen guessed that not too much time had elapsed. The sounds she was hearing were those of leave-taking. It was evidently still early enough so that people were heading off to work and to school.

The first of the morning rush hours would be over by now at the Day Care Centre. The working parents would already have dropped off their children, and the social mothers would not yet be into action.

What was Betty Smith doing now? Karen wondered. The drive to the Centre was a short one; the couple would have to have got there by now. Perhaps, at this very moment, Betty was being led on a grand tour of the building by Mrs Dunn or by Deedee.

'This is the kitchen,' one or the other of them would be telling her. 'That coffeepot's full; help yourself whenever you'd like a cup. That pan over there is the one we use for warming bottles for the babies.' . . . 'Here's the nursery room where Jane teaches.' . . . 'This is the room we call the Baby Room. It's where your niece works. You're such a lifesaver, Nancy, filling in for poor Karen today!'

Filling in for poor 'niece Karen', who, in reality, was not a relative at all – for Karen, who was not even 'sick', but who was lying, bound and gagged, on the floor of a deserted apartment.

This can't be happening, Karen thought incredulously. This is impossible!

Though her head still throbbed from its violent encounter with the stove corner, the intensity of the pain seemed to be lessening. As this occurred, Karen found herself becoming aware of other areas of discomfort. The twine with which

Betty's companion had tied her wrists and ankles was cutting into her badly, and her hands, which had been secured behind her back, were numb from the weight of her body. The dish towel pressed cruelly against her injured mouth, and her bones ached from her fall to the kitchen floor.

How long were they planning to leave her here? Karen wondered. What could the purpose behind all this be? If it was to rob the Centre, it was unlikely that Betty and her friend would be returning before evening. The parents paid when they picked their children up at night, not when they brought them in, and there was never much money in the cash drawer in the mornings. When it came to that, there was little money there at any time; most of the Centre's clients were regulars who paid monthly by cheque.

It simply didn't make sense. If this couple had decided to rob a business establishment, there were any number of more promising prospects. A bank or a store or even a video game hall would have more cash on hand. They had managed to learn everything else about the Centre – who was employed there, who the director was – even the schedule of the bus that Karen rode to work in the mornings. It was inconceivable that they could be stupid enough to believe that there would be enough money at a day care centre to be worth the risk involved in robbing it.

The apartment complex had by now grown quiet. Those who had early morning commitments had apparently gone to meet them, and the remaining tenants were probably still sleeping. Actually, Karen wondered if there *were* any tenants who hadn't gone to work. People who lived at a rundown place like the Tumbleweed were not likely to be in an income bracket that allowed them to sit around home all day.

The one person who could reasonably be expected still to be there was the manager. She tried to visualise the apartment with the vacancy sign in front of it. Betty had driven past it so quickly that she could not remember exactly where it had been located. It seemed to her that it had been near the east end of the complex. They had then turned right twice and had gone only a short way up the alley before they had pulled to a stop behind the laundry van.

That meant that the manager's apartment was close to this one. It might even be positioned directly next door. The manager would have pass keys to all the units. Was there a chance that he might go into them while the tenants were out?

It was a happy thought to contemplate, but, much as she longed to believe it might happen, Karen had to admit to herself that it was not likely. Betty had commented on the privacy that the complex afforded.

'The neighbours aren't snoopy,' she had said, 'and neither is the manager. If you pay your rent in advance, you can expect to go indefinitely without being bothered.'

What else had she said in the time they had spent together? Again, Karen found herself experiencing the feeling that she had missed something. Carefully, she reviewed every word she could remember. First, she and Betty had talked in the car. Then, the man, Jed, had entered the picture. He had dragged Karen into the apartment and called her a 'wildcat'. 'Surprise, surprise!' Betty had said. 'She doesn't look much like one, does she?' What else had she told him? 'Tie our little friend up, and let's get going. You did get gas, didn't you?'

Hold it a minute! What was that about the gas?

Karen slowed the pace of her mind and centred it upon that item.

'You did get gas?' Betty had asked – yet *she* had been the one who had been out that morning. If gas for the car had been needed, she would have bought it. The gas she was referring to must have been for the van. Did that mean that she had expected to drive the van to the Centre? That didn't seem reasonable. It would have looked strange for Karen's 'Aunt Nancy' to have arrived in a laundry truck. What was it, then, that the van was to be used for?

As she reviewed the conversation, Karen remembered that there had been a second part of it. After asking about gas, Betty had mentioned needing a road map. That had to mean that after the robbery, the pair was planning to head immediately for some place far enough away so that they needed a map in order to plan their route.

And, *that* must mean—

Dear God, Karen realised with sudden horror, *they're not coming back here!*

They were not going to release her – and why on earth should they? A return trip to the apartment would gain them nothing.

I'm going to be left here! I won't be discovered until next month's rent is due! Karen shuddered convulsively. *How long can I stay alive?*

She had read articles about people who had been marooned in wilderness areas, set adrift in lifeboats, or stranded in the desert. Some of them had survived for weeks without food, but in all cases such as those there had at least been water. Food was important, but water was more so. No one could live very long without liquid intake.

I've got to get out of here – but how?

Wincing with the pain the effort caused her, she tried to move her legs. Although she could lift them, it became quickly apparent that it would be hopeless to attempt to break the twine. It was looped several times around her ankles and knotted tightly.

Using her legs for balance, Karen raised her right shoulder and managed to roll partway over on to her left side. With the weight of her body now off her hands, she tried to restore the circulation in her fingers. They were so numb that it was impossible for her to tell if they were responding when she tried to wiggle them. The twine that bound her wrists was as tight as that around her ankles. She would never be able to slide it off, and there was nothing within reach that offered a sharp enough edge to cut it.

With a moan of defeat, she rolled back into her former position. It was obvious that she wouldn't be able to free herself. Her only hope was to attract the attention of someone in another apartment. Sound seemed to travel easily through the thin walls. If only she could find a way to create some really disturbing noise, there was a chance that one of the neighbours would complain to the manager.

The dish towel sealed her mouth as effectively as the twine held her ankles and wrists. The sole mobility she had was in her legs, and they could be lifted and lowered only as a unit. She tried raising them as high as possible and slamming them down against the floor. The impact was soaked up by the warped linoleum, and the resulting sound was only a muffled thud. Striking her feet against the stove front created a louder noise, but it was one that might easily have been mistaken for the rattle of defective plumbing. Still, doing anything had to be more constructive than doing nothing. Karen continued to kick the oven door, keeping up a steady, monotonous rhythm and praying that if she continued this effort long enough someone might begin to wonder about the repeated clanging.

Time passed; she couldn't gauge how much. Sounds in the alley changed as the morning moved onward. Several trucks pulled through, and one of them stopped for a few minutes to pick up garbage. There was a cat fight, and then some dogs staged a barking match. Some women strolled past, chatting idly, and Karen could hear the creak of the wheels of baby strollers.

Eventually, there came a burst of young voices, accompanied by laughter, and the doors of some of the apartment units banged open and shut again. It was noon,

Karen realised, and these were children who had come home to eat lunch.

By now her legs were exhausted, but she relentlessly continued to flail them against the stove front. No one seemed to notice or question the noise that resulted.

After what seemed hours, she again heard the sound of doors and voices. Lunch hour was apparently over. One boy shouted directly outside the kitchen window, his voice so loud and immediate that he might as well have been in the room with her. Somebody else jangled a bicycle bell. There were shrieks and giggles.

A shrill voice cried, 'Hey, guys, wait for me!'

Then, they were gone.

Wearily, Karen let her legs collapse on to the floor. She had been sustaining herself on hope and hiding from reality. Help was there, all right. It was only a matter of yards away in all directions, but she was not going to be able to attract it unless a miracle occurred.

She closed her eyes tightly, forcing back tears.

I *won't* cry! she told herself. I won't let myself go to pieces. I'll keep thinking – keep trying to find some answer – as long as I possibly can.

Then, something strange happened. Shut off from the world as she was by her own sealed eyelids, Karen experienced the sudden realisation that she was no longer alone. It was not as though she heard or felt anything definite, yet, she was aware of another presence in the kitchen.

She opened her eyes, and the child was there. It was *the child*, the elf from the garden. Although the little girl had her back towards her, Karen recognised her at once by the set of the small shoulders and the flood of cornsilk hair.

Help me! she tried to cry to her.

The only sound she could produce was a soft moaning deep in her throat.

The child did not acknowledge Karen's presence directly, but she did seem aware that someone was observing her.

Slowly, she tilted back her head and directed her gaze upwards toward the top of the kitchen doorway. She held this position until Karen looked up also and saw something that she had previously made little note of – the smoke alarm in the ceiling.

The smoke alarm! How could she not have thought of that! On the front of the stove there was a line of dials that activated the burners and two of them were within reach of her feet.

Quite suddenly, her legs felt tired no longer. Clumsy as the process would be, she was certain that if she worked at it long enough she would be able to manipulate the two nearest dials with the tip of one of her shoes.

The doorway was empty now. The child had gone. *But not too far.*

Karen raised her feet and began to prise at the dial that was situated nearest her. She had been kicking at it for several minutes when it occured to her that what she was attempting to do might be dangerous. From her prone position, there was no way that she could determine with any certainty whether the stove was gas or electric. If it was gas, and she kicked the vent open, she would be releasing poisonous vapour into the room

She assessed this possibility and then discarded it. Although she had nothing more than intuition upon which to base her assumption, she felt strangely confident that the stove was electric and that this escape scheme was going to work. She trusted the child; it was that simple. She felt a quiet sense of certainty that the little girl loved her and would do nothing that would hurt her.

Twisting her ankles, Karen struggled to work her feet into a better position to rotate the knob. She tried to recall if this was the burner across which her rain scarf had been thrown. She had been so frightened at the time that the scarf was ripped from her head that she hadn't taken notice of exactly where it had fallen.

Please, let this be it, she prayed. Let this be the one.

Time moved by slowly. The muted light in the kitchen grew even dimmer, and Karen became aware that in that foreign world beyond the curtained window it had once again resumed raining. Dampness seeped into the room, calling up other musty odours from cabinets and walls and warped linoleum. Neighbourhood children returned from school with a clatter of bikes and voices, and went banging and shouting into their home apartments. Television sets and record players went on. The sound of rock music slid through the walls and meshed with the beeps and shrieks of Atari tapes and the strident cartoon voices of 'Tom and Jerry'.

Karen continued to work at manipulating the dial.

She never knew the exact moment at which her purpose was accomplished. The room was so dim by then that she could no longer see what she was doing.

Her first indication of success was when she began to smell what she would afterwards remember as the most beautiful fragrance in the world – the acrid odour of wet and melting plastic.

14

It didn't surprise Karen to learn that the children were gone. It was as though, during the course of that endless and unbelievable day, she had reached a point at which nothing could ever surprise her again.

She listened stoically as a balding police officer named Sergeant Rice informed her of what had occurred.

'They took twelve children,' he told her, 'all of them infants. They had a laundry truck parked in the alley behind the building. A couple of people in the neighbourhood remember seeing it there, but they assumed it was making a delivery. The woman who was passing herself off as your aunt evidently let the man in through the back while her assistant was across the street getting a Coke. He carted those babies out like they were dirty linen. Then she got into the van with him, and they took off.'

'There was another car besides the van,' said Karen.

'We know about that. It's still parked in front of the Centre. We checked it out and found that it's a stolen vehicle. The owner lives in Dallas.'

They were talking in the Connors' living room. Karen's parents had refused to take her over to the Centre.

'That place is a madhouse,' said her mother. 'The police are dusting for fingerprints – parents are screaming and crying – Mrs Dunn is having hysterics. The last thing you need right now is to be exposed to all that.'

'You've been over there?' Karen asked her.

'Of course – for hours. I tried calling you around the middle of the morning and couldn't get in on the line. When it was still busy twenty minutes later, I got in the car and drove over to see what the matter was. The police had just got there. It was pure chaos even *then*!'

Now, at seven-thirty in the evening, Mrs Connors looked

almost as exhausted as Karen felt. Her eyes were bloodshot, and her face had a haggard, caved-in look.

'Are you finished with Karen now?' she asked the police sergeant. 'If so, she needs to get some rest.'

'I think we've covered everything.' Sergeant Rice consulted his notebook. 'Your daughter's description of the woman, "Betty", matches the one that was given us by the people at the Centre. Nobody else seems to have seen the man, "Jed", so in his case Karen's description is all we have to go on. Maybe somebody at the Tumbleweed can add something. We'll be interviewing the other tenants later this evening.'

'Let us know if there's anything we can do,' said Mr Connors. 'We're so grateful to have our own daughter home safe again. I can imagine the hell those other poor parents are going through.'

'The van was blue,' volunteered Karen. 'It had "Sanicare Laundry" printed on the side.'

'We'll get that out on the radio,' said Sergeant Rice. 'I imagine, though, that they've long since got rid of the lettering. It was probably put on with something that could be peeled right off.'

'I wish I'd thought to memorise the licence plate,' said Karen. 'Everything happened so fast. I realise now that I didn't do any of the things I should have.'

'You got yourself out,' the police sergeant reminded her. 'If you hadn't got the manager's attention by setting off that smoke alarm, you'd still be lying there in that kitchen two months from now. That's how far in advance those people had paid their rent.'

'She was incredibly lucky,' said Mr Connors.

'She made her own luck.' Sergeant Rice heaved himself up out of the depths of the armchair in which he had been sitting and got heavily to his feet. 'If you think of anything, Karen, that you haven't already told us, call immediately. Keep going back over things in your mind. Details that didn't seem worth noting at the time may turn out in the long run to be really important.'

They exchanged good nights, and Karen's father accompanied the police officer to the door.

The moment the two men were out of the room, Mrs Connors turned accusingly to her daughter.

'Since you were tiny, I've warned you against accepting rides from strangers. How could you have done such a stupid and dangerous thing?'

'It seemed so harmless,' said Karen. 'The woman looked nice and so sort of ordinary. She said she was trying to find the Centre, and, of course, that was right where I was going. It seemed natural to try to help her.'

'You could have died in that apartment,' said her mother. 'Did you hear what that policeman just said? It would have been months before anybody went in there and found you. It's a miracle that you're here and alive right now.'

'Yes, I know,' Karen agreed.

'And those poor little children!'

'Mom, I know I was responsible for this awful thing happening! You don't have to keep reminding me; I feel terrible enough already.' She regarded her mother miserably. 'I just can't keep talking about it. I'm going upstairs.'

'Don't you want some supper?' Mrs Connors asked her.

'I'm not hungry.'

'You need to eat something. I'll heat up some soup. We haven't any of us had anything to eat since breakfast.'

'All right,' Karen said, because it was easier to agree than to argue. 'First, though, I want a shower.'

She left the room quickly, in hopes of avoiding further discussion. When she reached the foot of the stairs, however, something occurred to her that caused her to pause. For a long moment she stood there, frozen, her hand already on the banister and one foot half raised to place on the lowest step.

Then, slowly, she lowered her foot, turned, and retraced her steps back down the hall to the living room.

Her mother was still seated on the sofa. Her shoulders were slumped, and she looked older than Karen could ever remember having seen her.

'Why did you try to call me?' Karen asked her.

Her mother's eyes sharpened. 'What do you mean?'

'You said that you phoned me at the Centre,' Karen said. 'You don't usually do that. What did you want me for?'

'I don't recall,' Mrs Connors said. 'It couldn't have been about anything important.'

'What were you doing when you decided to phone me?' When her mother didn't answer, Karen continued, 'Were you folding laundry?'

'Why do you ask a thing like that?'

'I saw you,' Karen said. 'Just as I fell, I saw you. You were standing in front of the clothes dryer, folding a bed sheet. You looked as though you'd just seen a ghost.'

'You and your visions!' Mrs Connors exclaimed in exasperation. 'Haven't they caused us enough unhappiness? I don't want to discuss that sort of thing any further, not now or ever.' She changed the subject. 'Which kind of soup do you want, chicken noodle or split pea?'

There was a moment's silence.

'Which kind?'

'Chicken,' Karen said wearily.

'I'm going to go ahead and start fixing supper,' her mother told her. 'Hurry up with your shower, or the food will be ready before you are.'

With a sigh of defeat, Karen re-entered the hall and ascended the stairs. Ensconced in the second-floor bathroom, she pulled off her blouse and skirt and let them drop to the tile floor. The smell of smoke and the sour stench of nervous perspiration almost overwhelmed her. Trying not to gag at the combination of odours, she gathered up the soiled clothes and stuffed them hastily into the laundry hamper. When she slammed down the lid, she told herself determinedly that she was sealing away the whole dreadful day.

She reached into the shower and turned on the water full volume, adjusting the temperature so that it ran as hot as she could stand it. Then she stepped into the steaming stall and stood beneath the torrent of water, rotating slowly so that the thin, fierce needles could stab at every pore of her skin.

The raw areas that the twine had scraped around her wrists and ankles felt as though they were being seared with acid. Glancing down at her upper right arm, she could see four purple bruises forming an even line against the pale skin. Directly opposite, and already turning an ugly yellow around the edges, there was a fifth bruise, slightly larger and darker than the others.

Karen shuddered and twisted her arm so that it was positioned directly under the stream of pounding water.

In her mind, she saw a blue van filled with babies. It wasn't a vision; it was simply a mental picture, and she refused to look at it.

I will *not* brood about the children, she told herself. It's not as though I can do a thing to help them. The police are out there searching. It's their responsibility. They're the ones with the authority and the manpower. They can radio out descriptions and set up roadblocks. Finding people is what they've been trained to do.

Finding people – the way they found Carla Sanchez?

No! Karen screamed silently in response to the monstrous question that rose from the teeming shadows at the back of her brain. *Nothing terrible is going to happen to those children. They haven't gone wandering off to fall in a river. People don't kidnap babies in order to kill them. They're alive and safe, and once ransom has been paid, they'll be returned to their parents.*

Desperate for another subject to think about, she focused

on the latest confrontation with her mother. It had been confusing. It was true, that her mother had been under a great deal of stress that day. That alone, however, could not have accounted for the way she had reacted when Karen had questioned her about her attempted phone call. Mrs Connors was not a person who did things on impulse. She had to have had a motive for calling the Centre, and Karen was sure that it had been triggered by whatever it was that had happened that morning in the laundry room. The expression of shock that she had seen on her mother's face in the vision she had experienced at the apartment had not been imagined. It had been very real.

What was it all about? Karen asked herself. What could it have been that her mother had witnessed, alone there as she had been, that had so frightened her that it had caused her to drop the sheet she was folding and rush to the telephone? And why, now, was she unwilling even to talk about it?

The water had by this time been running so long that it was barely tepid, and Karen's skin had begun to wrinkle. She was trying to decide whether or not to get out of the shower when the decision was taken from her by a rap on the bathroom door and the muffled sound of her mother's voice attempting to call something to her over the noise of the running water.

Karen twisted the faucet dial to the off position and opened the door of the shower stall.

'Yes, what is it?' she called back.

'You'd better dry off and get dressed,' her mother told her. 'A policeman's here, and he wants to talk with you.'

'I thought we were finished,' said Karen. 'I told him everything I could think of.'

'This isn't Sergeant Rice,' said her mother. 'It's that other one – what was his name? – Officer Wilson. It's the man who drove you out to the Valley to look for the Sanchez girl. He says there's something he needs to discuss with you in private.'

'I can't imagine what it could be,' said Karen. 'I've already given all the information I have to Sergeant Rice.'

'I told him that,' said Mrs Connors. 'I also told him you were exhausted and not up to seeing anybody unless it was absolutely necessary. He won't go away. He says this is important.'

Karen drew a deep breath.

'OK,' she said reluctantly. 'Tell him I'll be down in a few minutes.'

The silence that followed was so prolonged that she was beginning to think that her mother had left to go back downstairs, when Mrs Connors spoke again.

'You probably do have to talk with him. He does represent the law. There's no reason, though, that I can see, why any police officer needs to interrogate a young girl in private. I think it's your right to have your parents with you.'

If the statement had been put in the form of a question – 'Do you want Dad and me to be with you when you talk with him?' – Karen's response would have been immediate and positive. She had no desire to see Ron Wilson again at all, much less to be alone with him.

As usual, however, her mother's presumptive attitude aroused automatic obstinacy.

'I'll see him alone, if that's what he wants,' Karen told her.

'I don't think he has the right—'

'I told you, Mom, it's OK,' Karen said, interrupting the protest. 'I'll be down in a couple of minutes.'

She stepped out of the shower stall and instantly started shivering. It was as though all the warmth in her body had been drained away in the course of the short conversation. She dried herself hurriedly, towelling the water from her hair, but not taking time to use the dryer. The lank strands still hung damp upon her shoulders as she went into the bedroom and hastily dressed in a T-shirt and a pair of jeans.

When she went downstairs to the living room, Ron Wilson was there waiting for her. Her parents were nowhere to be seen. One look at the young policeman's face brought fear sweeping over her.

'What's happened?' Karen asked in panic. 'Have the children been found? Are they all right?'

'No, they haven't been found, so I don't know if they're all right or not.' The pain in his eyes belied the crispness of the statement. 'How are you feeling? Did they hurt you?'

'Not really,' said Karen. 'I have a few bruises and a headache.'

'The report that came into the station said a young woman was missing as well as the children. I didn't know at first that it was you. Then somebody mentioned the name "Connors", and I remembered that you'd said you worked at a day centre.' He paused, and then said accusingly, 'You never returned my phone calls.'

'I didn't want to talk about Carla Sanchez,' Karen told him. 'I wanted to be able to forget her.'

'I can understand how you'd feel that way,' Ron said. 'The thing is, it's not going to be that easy. You can't get away from an experience like that one. It's bound to follow you. Today – those kids—'

'I didn't make this happen!' Karen broke in defensively. 'The kidnapping wasn't planned around me personally. Those people had it all set up. They would have gone through with it anyway, no matter who was in charge of the Baby Room.'

'That's probably true,' Ron acknowledged. 'Whether it was a coincidence or not, though, the fact is that you *were* the one in charge, and you *were* the one who was taken. You got to see the couple, the man as well as the woman. You've had personal contact with the kids. If you were able to locate Carla when you didn't even know her—'

'No!' Karen exploded. 'I'm not going to try that again. You can't know what that experience was like for me. If you did, you'd never even suggest it.'

'Will you do me one favour?' Ron asked her. 'Will you take an hour and come with me to talk with somebody?'

'Not if it's a parent of one of the children,' said Karen. 'I can't take that. It would be like reliving that morning at the Sanchezes'.'

'This isn't one of the parents. It's Anne Summers.'

'The psychic you told me about?' Karen regarded him with surprise. 'I thought she was supposed to be in Dallas.'

'She was,' Ron said. 'She's back now.'

'Then why don't you get *her* to track down the children?' Karen demanded. 'That's what she does, isn't it? That's her profession.'

'That's not her profession,' Ron said shortly. 'Anne donates her services, without charge, because she feels it's her duty. She'd be helping us this time, if she could, but she's in the hospital. Two nights ago, somebody shot her.'

15

The chair outside the door to Anne Summers's hospital room was occupied by a uniformed policeman. He and Ron seemed to know each other and exchanged greetings.

'How's she doing?' Ron asked.

'OK, I guess,' the other officer told him. 'The doctor was in and out a while ago. He says this is one tough lady.'

'We knew that already.'

'Yeah, but, tough or not, it's no fun stopping a bullet. It's damned lucky she was holding that sack in front of her.'

Ron nodded in agreement. 'Is there anybody in there with her?'

'Not at the moment,' the other man said. 'Her husband left right after you did to get some dinner. Their son was here for most of the afternoon, and he's coming back later. The doc's cracking down on visitors. He says that, just because she's out of intensive care, it doesn't mean she can handle a lot of talking.'

'This is Karen Connors,' Ron told him. 'Mrs Summers asked specifically to see her.'

'Have you checked with the doc about it?' the man asked doubtfully. 'I don't want to be caught in the middle on this one. You're not even on duty now, are you?'

'There won't be a problem,' Ron assured him. 'We're only going to be here a couple of minutes.'

Before the discussion could proceed any further, he rapped on the door, hastily shoved it open, and stepped inside, motioning to Karen to follow him.

The room that they entered was decorated in standard hospital style, with stainless steel furniture, pale green walls, and white, double-layered draperies sheathing the window. A single bed on rollers jutted out from one wall, and there was a curtain drawn partway around it. A shelf along the top of the opposite wall held a potted plant and two vases of multicoloured flowers. An inactive television set was positioned on a raised stand directly across from the bed.

Ron pushed the door gently closed behind them. The click of the latch falling into place seemed startlingly loud.

There was a moment of silence.

Then, Ron said softly, 'Anne? Are you awake?'

'Is that you, Ronnie?' The voice that responded was low-pitched and hoarse, as though it had not been used for a while. 'I'm awake, but not for long, I'm afraid. They've fed me some pills. Were you able to bring the girl?'

'She's right here,' Ron said.

'Well, get her over where I can see her. It's – Karen – isn't it?'

'That's right,' Ron said. 'Karen Connors.' He put his hand on Karen's arm and drew her over to the opening in the curtain.

The woman who lay in the bed on the far side of it was singularly unremarkable in appearance. She had a round, pleasant face, wide-spaced hazel eyes that seemed to be struggling to focus, and a mouth that was a bit too large to synchronise with her other features. The hair that lay spread across the pillow was chestnut colour and lightly frosted with grey.

'Well, here she is,' Ron said. 'This is Karen. Karen, meet Anne Summers, my tenth-grade English teacher.'

'Your teacher!' exclaimed Karen. 'You never told me that!'

'I told you I'd known her since high school.'

'Yes, but I thought – I mean, I took it for granted – that what you meant was that you'd been students together. Teachers aren't – they aren't supposed to be—'

'They aren't supposed to be psychics?' Anne Summers's

gravelly voice completed the statement. 'Is that a rule you've learned somewhere? If so, please, tell me about it.'

'I'm sorry,' Karen said in embarrassment. 'I didn't mean to sound so stupid. I was surprised, that's all. You aren't what I expected.'

'I knew what you meant,' the woman told her. 'I was giving you a hard time, that's all. I'm good at that, aren't I, Ronnie? I gave Ron a hard time, nonstop, for the two semesters I had him in my class. He was a difficult student, always wanting to spell things his own way. I wouldn't let him get away with it.'

'That's enough of that,' Ron said lightly. 'I didn't bring Karen here so you could tell her I was a rotten teenager.'

'No, of course, you didn't,' Anne Summers said. 'You brought her so I could get a look at her. Can you help me find my glasses? I can't imagine where that nurse could have put them.'

'Are these them?' Ron picked up a pair of wire-rimmed bifocals that lay in plain sight on the bedside table.

'These are *they*,' the woman corrected him. 'It's humiliating to have such poor eyesight that you can't see to find your glasses unless you're wearing them.' She reached up to take them from him, and Karen saw that her hand was shaking.

'I don't know why I'm so much weaker tonight,' Anne said apologetically, as she fumbled the glasses into place on the rim of her nose. 'It's probably too much bed rest. I'm not used to that. Step nearer, Karen, so I can get a real look at you. Ron was right; you certainly are pretty. How old are you?'

'Eighteen,' Karen told her, flushing at the unexpected compliment.

'That's the age I was when I took on *my* first case.'

'I'm not taking on a case,' Karen said quickly. 'I don't know what Ron's told you, but I'm not a real psychic the way you are. There was a mix-up about what went into the paper.'

'Ron's told me all about that,' said Anne Summers. 'The mix-up was in the fact that the article got into the paper at all, not in the story itself. You did find the child who was missing, didn't you?'

'She was dead,' Karen said. 'She'd drowned in the river. My finding her was no kindness to anybody. It would have been better if she *hadn't* been found.'

'That's not true,' Anne said. 'Not knowing – that's the ultimate nightmare. Can you imagine what life must be like for parents who wait month after month, year after year, for children who never return? The poor child's mother had to be permitted to let go of hope. Still, it's painful, always so painful, when a search ends in tragedy. You will never fully get used to that, Karen. With time, though, you will grow strong enough to bear it.'

'I don't *want* to grow that strong!' Karen exclaimed. 'I don't *want* to be a psychic!'

'Of course you don't,' said Anne Summers. 'It's a hellish responsibility, being born with a third eye. There's a theory that psychic ability's an inherited trait. My grandmother had the gift.'

'Well, I'm sure mine didn't,' said Karen, 'or my mother would have told me about it. And, however it is that people come to have one, I don't consider a third eye a "gift".'

'You might as well, dear,' Anne said reasonably. 'From what Ron's told me, you're very definitely endowed with one. You'll find it pleasanter, under the circumstances, to think of it as a gift than as a curse.'

'We're not going to be allowed to stay very long,' said Ron. 'If there are things you want Karen to know—'

'Yes, let's get down to business.' Anne spoke with sudden briskness. 'As you can see, Karen, I'm out of commission. It's a miracle, in fact, that I'm even alive. After dinner, the other evening, I turned on the outside light and stepped out the kitchen door to carry out the rubbish. Someone was waiting in the shadows at the corner of the house. As luck would have it, the sack I was carrying contained a broken meat grinder. That slowed the force of the bullet and deflected it.'

Karen regarded the woman incredulously. 'What sort of maniac would shoot somebody without any reason!'

'There was a reason,' Anne said. 'I was becoming too much of a threat. I'd been getting too close – learning too much.'

'I told you about the kidnapping in Dallas,' Ron said to Karen. 'That's the case Anne's been working on.'

'The vibes were strong,' Anne said. 'That was one of those cases where the feelings just kept *coming*. I didn't even have to reach for them. I stood in that nursery next to those empty cribs, and it was as though the children were still in them. I could even see the couple who had taken them. If I were able to help with this new investigation, I'm almost certain I could find them.'

Karen stared at her.

'You mean you think those Texas people took our babies also?'

'Yes, I do,' Anne said. 'The situations are so similar. With the Texas kidnapping, both a man and a woman were involved. They worked as a team, with the woman infiltrating the nursery and the man doing the driving. Ron says it was that way here.'

'What did the couple look like?' Much as she hated to be drawn any further into this, Karen found herself incapable of turning from it. 'Was anyone at the nursery able to describe them?'

'They never saw the man,' Anne said. 'My feeling is that he was heavyset and had a beard. The members of the nursery staff who had contact with the woman guessed her to be in her late thirties. She wore a bandana which hid her hair colour. I feel sure, though, that it was red.'

'Then, they couldn't have been the same couple,' said Karen. 'The man who tied me up *was* bearded, but the woman's hair was almost exactly the shade of mine.'

'The woman was a redhead,' Anne repeated with certainty. 'Perhaps she's dyed it to fake a family resemblance to you, but its natural colour is red. The car they were driving was some sort of truck. No – strike that. Actually, I think, it was more of a bus or a van. It was blue, and the people had put mattresses in the back.'

'You think the couple in Dallas drove a van?' Karen shot a startled glance at Ron. 'Those people today were driving a blue van.'

'I know that,' Ron said, 'but I didn't tell Anne.'

'There were mattresses,' Anne repeated, ignoring his interruption. Behind the thick lenses of her glasses, her eyelids were fluttering strangely and her voice had changed. It had taken on a rich, crooning quality that sounded the way woodsmoke smelled. 'They drove those babies a long, long way. They took them into another state. When I looked into my mind to try to find them, I saw a mountain rising above a string of foothills. There was snow on its peak. You don't find scenery like that in Texas. There is a house, and the children fall asleep there to the sound of rushing water. There aren't as many there now as there once were. People keep taking them.'

The doorknob rattled.

Startled, Karen turned in time to see the door thrown open. A tall grey-haired man in hospital whites stood in the doorway.

His face was flushed, and his eyes were bright with anger.

'What are you people doing here? Only immediate family has access to this room.'

'I'm Officer Ronald Wilson,' Ron began defensively. 'We're conducting an investigation—'

'I know who you are,' the man said icily. 'I met you with Police Chief Robinson. In case you've forgotten, *I* am Dr

Prior, the surgeon who removed a bullet from this woman's abdomen. I informed you earlier, and I am now informing you again, that my patient is in no condition to have visitors.'

'I asked them to come,' Anne volunteered.

'Mrs Summers is a psychic,' said Ron. 'We think the person who shot her was trying to keep her from helping the police.'

'Then, he's done what he set out to do,' said Dr Prior. 'As Mrs Summers's physician, I care more about her health than about your investigation. Besides that, I was present this afternoon when Chief Robinson informed you that you were being removed from the kidnapping case. You have no authority to be in this room, and I want you out of here.'

'Anne,' Ron said, 'I'm sorry.'

'That's OK,' Anne said. 'I couldn't have talked much longer anyway. Thanks for bringing your friend. Karen – good luck to you. Sleep well tonight, and dream.'

'Good night,' Karen said. 'I hope you're better soon.'

Out in the hospital corridor, the uniformed policeman, who had been so friendly upon their arrival, was now bristling with hostility.

'You gave me a snow job, Wilson,' he said accusingly. 'You didn't tell me you were off this case. You can be damned sure the minute he's out of that room the doc will be on the phone to Robinson.'

'I had to go in there,' Ron told him. 'It was important that I see Mrs Summers. You don't need to get stuck with the blame. Say I lied and bluffed my way past you.'

'Rookie cops don't decide what's important,' the other man said. 'If you join the force, you play by the rules.'

'Then, maybe I shouldn't be on it,' said Ron. 'If the Chief wants to talk to me, I'll be over at my brother's.'

He reached for Karen's arm, got a death grip on it, and began to propel her rapidly down the corridor towards the elevators. The clock on the wall by the nurses' station read eight thirty-seven. Visiting hours were now in full swing, and flower-and-candy-laden people poured past them in a steady stream. From the open doorways on either side of the hall there came the murmur of live voices, blended with the canned discord of an assortment of television programmes.

'Slow down,' Karen said. 'Please, Ron, I can't keep up with you.'

For a moment, she thought he was going to ignore her. Then, abruptly, he slowed his stride and released his hold on her arm.

'I'm sorry,' he said gruffly. 'I'm mad as hell, but not at you.'

'If it was that doctor who made you so angry—'

'It wasn't,' Ron said. 'Not the man himself, I mean. He was doing his job. It was the timing of it – having him burst in like that at just the point when Anne was really getting rolling.'

'She was worn out,' said Karen. 'We were pushing her too hard.'

'I don't think we were. She wanted to talk. It was the medication that was making her groggy.'

'Why did you do it?' asked Karen. 'Why did you bring me here, when you knew you weren't supposed to? Why pretend you're assigned to this case if you really aren't?'

They were standing now in front of the row of elevators. Ron reached across and gave a vicious punch to the 'Down' button.

'Anne asked me to bring you,' Ron said. 'I'd told her about your finding Carla. She said then that she wanted to meet you. When this happened today, it made it imperative. Anne can't work, and you can.'

'But you're off the case now,' said Karen. 'At least, that's what the doctor said. Is that the truth?'

'Yes,' Ron admitted, 'but what does that matter? I knew

Anne Summers long before the Police Department ever even heard of her. I can talk with her as a friend and former student.'

'That's not how it was, though,' said Karen. 'You came to my house tonight in uniform. You made it sound as though you were there on official business.'

'I had to,' Ron said, without apology. 'If I hadn't, your parents would never have let you come with me.'

'But, you had no right—'

'I *do* have a right!' Ron said belligerently. 'I'm involved in this! I don't need to be authorised by *anybody*!'

Karen stared at him in bewilderment.

'You care so much?'

'You're damned right, I care!' Ron told her. 'Matthew Wilson is my nephew!'

16

'Sleep well tonight, and dream!'

It did not happen immediately. For the early part of the night Karen lay comatose, drugged by sheer fatigue, sunk in deep drifts of sleep so thick and all-encompassing that they provided insulation from the world. In the later hours, however, she slid from a condition of total oblivion into a second state of slumber. It was at this point that the dreams that had been lying coiled beneath her pillow began to emerge.

The first of the images were not her own. A snowcapped mountain loomed ahead of her, but it was not her mountain, it was Anne's; and the house that lay beyond it was the house that Anne had described to her. The van parked out to the side had no letters on it. It was the van that Anne had envisioned, and the floor of it was covered with mattresses.

Karen thought, at first, that the river might be Anne's as well. Viewed, rippling and swirling, from a distance, it might have been any wild river, drunk on the juices of springtime. As she drew nearer, however, she began to see that what had originally appeared to her to be froth was composed of tiny white bodies clad in diapers and nightgowns. It was then that she knew that this river had not been inspired by one of Anne Summers's visions. A pair of child-sized sandals lay on its pebbled beach.

It was the sound of the river that woke her. The rush of water, cascading over rocks, tugging at tree roots, hurling itself against the bank and bouncing back again, was horribly familiar. The noise rose in her ears to a thunderous roar and threw her violently awake.

Cast up so abruptly on to the shores of consciousness, Karen was too shaken to think past the pounding of her heart. It had been a dream, she tried to reassure herself, not a vision. The two were distinctly different. Visions depicted reality, but dreams were imaginary. It would have been strange, indeed, if the events of the previous day had not triggered at least one good, old-fashioned nightmare.

Forcing her mind away from the spectacle of the child-spattered river, she transferred her gaze from the bedroom ceiling to the window. Beyond the pane, the sun was shining, but the pearl-coloured sky was still smeared with the remnants of yesterday's rainstorm. The diffused brilliance produced an eerie glitter that seemed to fill the air with flickering silver.

For a long time, Karen lay quiet, letting herself become semihypnotized by the oscillating patterns of the shifting light. Finally, she forced herself to sit up in bed. The effort it took to haul herself into a sitting position brought home to her how much abuse her body had taken. Tentatively, she felt for the spot on her head that had struck the stove corner. It was puffy and sore to the touch. The smudged yellow bruises that lay exposed below the sleeve of her summer pyjamas were additional ugly reminders of the previous day's adventure.

Painfully, Karen dragged herself out of bed. When she went downstairs, she found her mother at the kitchen table, drinking coffee and reading the paper.

'So you're up!' Mrs Connors said by way of greeting. 'I thought you'd sleep a lot longer. How are you feeling?'

'Sore,' Karen told her. 'I ache all over, especially my legs.'

'I bet you're hungry,' her mother said. 'You ate so little yesterday. What would you like for breakfast? There's bacon and eggs, or, if you like, I can make French toast.'

'Eggs would be fine.' Karen eyed the newspaper apprehensively. 'I suppose it made the front page?'

'Of course,' said Mrs Connors, getting up from the table. 'Where would you expect it to be? They even have a picture-spread on the children. It's disgusting the way those newspaper people insist on wringing every drop of drama out of people's heartache. There's one bright spot, though; they don't seem to have made the connection yet that you're the same Karen Connors who found Carla Sanchez.'

'I'm glad of that,' said Karen.

She picked up the paper and spread it out on the table. An array of familiar infant faces gazed up at her. In the bottom right corner of the lineup, a round-cheeked Matthew Wilson beamed engagingly. The picture was a standard department-store photograph, shot against an artificial backdrop of autumn foliage. Unlike the photos of some of the other babies, this one appeared to have been taken quite recently, for the dimple-to-dimple grin displayed his current four teeth.

'See this baby?' Karen held up the paper. 'He's Ron Wilson's nephew.'

'You mean, that policeman's related to one of the children?' said her mother in surprise. 'That explains, then, why he's so wrapped up in this case. He's already phoned you once this morning. He left his number and wants you to call back.'

'Did he say what he wanted?'

'No, but he did say there haven't been any ransom demands.'

'I can't understand that,' said Karen. 'It makes no sense. Why would anyone kidnap children except for ransom? This is the same thing that happened in Dallas. None of the parents there were contacted either.'

'Why do you mention that?' her mother asked her. 'Do the police think the two cases are connected?'

'Yes,' said Karen. 'Anne Summers, the woman Ron took me to visit at the hospital, was the psychic who worked on the case in Dallas. She feels that the kidnappings were committed by the same people.'

'The ones who shot her?'

There was a moment of silence.

Then Karen asked softly, 'How did you know that? How did you know that Anne was shot?'

'You mentioned it last night when you left for the hospital.'

'I'm sure that I didn't!'

'You must have,' her mother said logically. 'How else would I know? Doesn't that prove to you that you're playing with fire here? Involvement in this sort of thing is dangerous!'

'I know,' said Karen. 'Mom, believe me, I'm scared by it too.'

'Then, why take the risk? Why not leave town for a while?' Mrs Connors was standing at the stove now, with her back towards Karen. She lifted an egg and brought it down with a sharp crack against the edge of the frying pan. 'We could take a little trip.'

'You mean, you'd go with me?'

'I suggested it to your father at breakfast,' said her mother. There was a sizzling sound as the egg slid into hot bacon grease. 'What I was thinking was that you and I might visit San Francisco. There are all sorts of things to do in a city like that. The stores are fantastic, and we do need to get you clothes for college.'

'But I have a job,' Karen protested. 'I can't just take off. The Centre's understaffed. That's why Betty was able to get in there.'

'I've already spoken with Mrs Dunn,' said Mrs Connors. 'She called last night while you were out. She wanted to know how you were feeling and said to tell you that she's temporarily closing the centre. Actually, I don't think she has any alternative after all this negative publicity.'

'That's not fair!' exclaimed Karen. 'Mrs Dunn wasn't to blame for what happened!'

'Legally, she was. Those children were her responsibility.' Mrs Connors slid the eggs from the pan on to a plate and placed bacon strips beside them. 'About our trip,' she continued as she brought the food to the table and placed it in front of Karen. 'Don't you think it might be fun?'

'I don't want to have fun,' Karen told her. 'There's no way I can enjoy a vacation trip right now.'

'Don't be difficult, Karen,' said her mother. 'If you don't want to think of it as "fun", then think of it as self-protection. Just because reporters so far have missed the connection between Karen-the-Kidnapped and Karen-the-Psychic doesn't mean that they're going to keep on missing it. Soon, now, somebody will put two and two together. When that happens, it will be front-page news. You know how it was before, with all those letters and phone calls. Can you imagine how much worse it will be this time, when the missing children are all of them from here?'

'I hadn't thought of that,' said Karen. She had taken some food onto her fork. Now, she lowered it to her plate, untouched. 'It will be terrible.'

'There's also real physical danger,' said her mother. 'If those people felt so threatened by Anne Summers that they tried to kill her, how will they react when they find out that you have similar abilities? I should think they would consider you an even greater threat, because you've had personal contact with them.'

'OK,' Karen said. 'OK, Mom, you've convinced me. We'll go to San Francisco.'

'Good,' said her mother with satisfaction. 'I'm glad you're being sensible. I'll phone your father and see what sort of plane and hotel reservations he's been able to make for us.'

'You seem to have been pretty certain I'd go along with this.' Karen was unable to keep the edge of resentment from her voice.

'I was sure you'd realize you had no choice.' Her mother frowned as she consulted her watch. 'There are so many things to be done. I have a hair appointment at ten. I should be out of that by eleven-thirty, and I'll go by the bank and buy travellers' cheques. On the way home, I'll stop at the cleaners'.'

'We're going *today*?' Karen exclaimed incredulously. 'How long will we stay?'

'As long as we have to,' said her mother. 'That's why I'm picking up the cleaning. Since we can't be sure how long we'll be away, we should take an assortment of clothing. If it doesn't seem right to come home after San Francisco, we can stay with my cousin Ashley in Los Altos. She's always begging us to come visit in her Christmas notes.'

'What do you want me to do?' Karen asked.

'As soon as you've eaten, you'd better start packing,' her mother told her. 'If the phone rings, don't answer; it might be a reporter. I don't think you should answer the doorbell either. There's no sense taking risks. I'm carrying my keys, of course, and I'll lock as I go out.'

This is crazy, Karen told herself in the oppressive silence that followed her mother's departure. It's all of it crazy. Everything's happening too fast.

Her stomach was churning. Getting up from the table, she carried her plate to the sink and scraped the meat strips and globs of yellow egg yolk down the disposal. Then she left the kitchen and went down the hall to the storage closet where the family suitcases were kept. She chose one of these at random, carried it up the stairs to her room, and set it on the bed.

What should she pack? she wondered. Dresses were probably most appropriate for San Francisco. Would there be a pool where they would be staying? Yes, probably. She would want a swimming suit, then, and some shorts and T-shirts.

She crossed to the closet and stood, staring in at the rows of dresses and blouses. After considering for a moment, she selected several dresses, took them down from their hangers, and carried them over to the bed.

When she returned to the closet, her eyes fell upon the ivory lace Prom gown that hung towards the back, protected by a plastic dry-cleaners' bag. Should she pack that also? It was too dressy for most normal occasions, but in a city like San Francisco it might be different.

Karen started to reach for the dress and, then, hesitated. Suddenly, the whole scene seemed disconcertingly familiar. It was as though she were experiencing a replay of something that she had lived through once before. She had stood like this at a closet on another occasion, and had gazed in through the open door. There had been cotton dresses there – a jacket of some kind – and a lacy gown in a plastic bag. She had taken the dress from the bag and held it against her cheek. She had closed her eyes and—

Oh, God, she thought in a flash of horrified realization. It's not a Prom gown that I'm remembering!

The nausea that had threatened her in the kitchen came rushing back in a vicious surge. Wheeling away from the closet, she threw herself on to the bed and buried her face in the pillow. In the churning darkness the row of Carla's dresses flapped and fluttered as though caught in a windstorm, with the First Communion dress flying like a banner above them all. Gradually, like objects from *Fantasia*, they began to change in shape and size until they were infant clothing – tiny undershirts and kimonos.

It's happening, Karen thought wildly. It's happening again, and I can't stop it!

Mercilessly, the visions swept in upon her, and she was no longer in her bedroom, but speeding down a highway. The low, golden light of late afternoon slanted in through the window and fell warm against her left shoulder. Beyond the glass, there lay a strange landscape composed of rose-coloured rocks that stabbed at the cloudless sky like jagged spears. Beyond those, in the far distance, she could see a mountain with snow on its peak.

It was the man who was doing the driving. Karen saw

him as though she herself were riding in the back seat. The woman, Betty, sat beside him, studying a road map. When viewed from this angle, it was evident that her pale blonde hair had orange roots.

Karen could not see the children, but she could hear them crying somewhere behind her in the depths of the van. She could smell soiled diapers and the faint, sour odour of curdled milk. She could hear—

She could hear a telephone.

The reality of the jarring, repetitive shriek snapped open her eyes. The speeding van, the snowcapped mountain, the surrealistic pink rock formations were gone as quickly as they had materialized, and she was back on her bed, sprawled next to an open suitcase. The sky beyond the window was not clear and blue as the sky outside the van had been; it was iridescent and glimmering and sheeted over by a thin layer of misty clouds.

The phone continued to ring.

Responding automatically, Karen got up from the bed and went out into the hall. She had the receiver halfway to her ear when her mother's warning came back to her: 'If the phone rings, don't answer it.'

Habit was so deeply ingrained, however, that she did so anyway.

'Hello?'

'Karen? It's Ron,' said a familiar voice. 'I tried to reach you earlier, but your mother said you were still sleeping.'

'She told me you called,' Karen said. 'I hadn't had time to phone back yet. Things around here are pretty rushed right now. We're going on a trip.'

'*Who's* going on a trip?'

'My mother and I are,' said Karen. 'We're going to California. Mom thinks it would be better for me not to be here when the newspapers find out that I'm the same girl who located Carla.'

'When are you leaving?' Ron asked her.

'This afternoon,' said Karen. 'Will you, please, tell Anne Summers something for me? She was right in the things she told us last night. I saw it too today – that mountain with the snow. And Betty's natural hair colour is red, just as Anne said it was.'

'You saw them?' exclaimed Ron. 'You saw the children?'

'I didn't *see* them,' Karen told him, 'but I could *hear* them. We were out on the highway, and they were in the back of the van.'

'Which way were you headed?'

'I don't know.'

'Think!' Ron commanded. 'They must have left here with the kids some time around midday. That means they were driving during the afternoon. In your vision, was the sun at your right or your left?'

'My left,' Karen said, beginning to see his intention. 'That means – it *must* mean, then – that they were headed north.'

'And there was a mountain? Could you identify it?'

'No, I couldn't. There are so many mountains north of here, and it might have been any one of them. It could have been anywhere in northern New Mexico or Colorado or in Utah or even in California.'

'What else did you see?' Ron pressed her. 'There had to be something – a bridge – a road sign – railroad tracks. Were you passing through a town?'

'I didn't see buildings,' said Karen. 'All around us, though, there were pink rocks.'

'Pink rocks,' Ron echoed. He sounded excited. 'That gives us a base to work from. If we head north and keep our eyes open, we should be able to spot a place like that.'

'Ron, no!' Karen said. 'I told you, Mom and I are leaving.'

'But, you can't leave now,' Ron objected. 'You can't just walk out on this.'

'I've told you everything I know,' said Karen. 'I saw a

mountain and some funny-coloured rocks. I don't have any idea what those two things add up to. If anybody can make sense out of it, Anne can.'

'That's not an option,' Ron said. 'Not after last night. Dr Prior has that room sealed up like a bank vault. Nobody gets in there now except her husband and son. Don't you feel any sense of responsibility about this, Karen? You're the one who hitched a ride in that woman's car. If it weren't for you, she'd never have got access to the kids.'

'You're just trying to make me feel guilty!' Karen said accusingly.

'You *are* guilty!' Ron shot back at her. 'It was unintentional, sure, but you did make a dumb mistake. Don't you owe it to those kids and their parents to help undo it?'

'You're making me feel terrible!'

'That's my intention. You know what I'm saying is true, and you don't want to hear it.' Ron paused. 'Karen? Are you listening? I'll be over to pick you up in twenty minutes. My nephew is out there somewhere with those two creeps. This isn't just any kid I'm talking about, this is *Matthew!*'

Karen took the receiver from her ear and held it away from her. Ron's voice kept coming, hollow and strange, from its new vantage point.

'Karen? Do you hear me?'

She could not fight it.

'Come on over,' Karen said. 'I'll be ready when you get here.'

17

By the time dusk fell, they had been driving north for over seven hours. Ron had taken the Interstate up through northern New Mexico in to Colorado, pausing at junctions to turn questioningly to Karen.

'Should we take this side road? Do you think they might have turned off here? Should we continue to keep to the highway?'

'I don't know,' Karen told him repeatedly. 'I don't have any feelings about this at all.'

The visions that had on previous occasions arrived unbidden and unlonged-for now seemed to have deserted her entirely. Scenery slid past the car window, the sagebrush and mesquite bushes of the dry southwestern flatlands giving way to the pines and aspen of higher altitudes. Hills grew more rugged and eventually became the foothills that bordered mountains. None of these was capped with snow.

The sun slid slowly down the blue slope of sky and disappeared in the late afternoon behind a mountain ridge. The road was bathed in shadows, but the sky itself remained light for several more hours, reflecting the brilliance of the now hidden sun. Enough light still lingered to form a pale, violet-tinted dusk, when Ron at last pulled into a parking lot in front of a roadside diner.

'We'd better stop and get something to eat,' he said wearily. 'It's been a long drive up here, and there's the same distance to cover going back tonight. We both need a break and some food.'

'You mean, you're planning to turn around now and go home?' Karen's relief was tinged with irritation. 'You're giving up already?'

'What is it you *want* me to do?' Ron fired back at her.

'I hauled you up here under duress. You didn't expect it to lead to anything, and so of course it hasn't. I might as well take you home so you can go on your vacation trip.'

'That's not fair,' Karen said resentfully. 'You're making it sound as though I'm deliberately holding out on you. I want to find those children as much as you do.'

'How could you? Matt's not *your* nephew!' There was a moment of silence. Then Ron leaned back in the seat and rubbed furiously at his eyes with his knuckles. 'I'm sorry. You didn't deserve to get snarled at like that. I'm tired and disappointed, and I'm taking it out on you. Let's go in and get some supper, OK?'

He opened the door and got out of the car, and Karen, too upset to acknowledge the apology, got out also and followed him in silence into the restaurant. Once they were seated opposite each other in a booth, however, there was no place to look except straight into his face. The worry and exhaustion she saw reflected there extinguished her anger as quickly as his words had ignited it.

'I did really try,' she said.

'I told you, I'm sorry I flared up at you. I know you can't help it if the magic vibes aren't hitting right. I can see now why the Chief took me off this case. It's too close, too personal. I can't be objective and keep my cool; not when one of the missing kids is Steve's and Susie's.'

'I thought you resented your brother,' said Karen. 'Isn't he the family favourite, the one with the "golden touch"?'

'Did I tell you that?' Ron regarded her incredulously. Then he gave a short mirthless laugh. 'I can't believe I actually said that. It's something I haven't wanted to admit even to myself.'

'It's true, though, isn't it?'

'Yeah, it's true enough. There have been times when I've resented Steve so much that I've come close to hating him. Steve's the reason I joined the Police Force.'

'What do you mean?' asked Karen. 'Was a career in police work something you'd always wanted?'

'Nope, never. I planned on being a lawyer. My dad's an attorney who specializes in criminal law, and ever since I was a kid I've wanted to be just like him. That was the one area where I felt one up on Steve; I knew what I was going to do with my life, and he didn't. Steve had so many talents, he didn't know what to do with them all. One day he was going to be a surgeon; the next, an engineer; the next, an astronaut. There wasn't a doubt but that he'd make it big at anything he went into. He was straight-A in high school, the star of the football team, Student Body President. He had all the qualifications for anything.'

'And he decided on law?'

'Bang – out of the blue – without even thinking about it. That's how it seemed, anyway. We were both in college; Steve was a senior and I was a sophomore. Steve was majoring in political science or some such thing. Whatever it was, he had a 4.0 GPA. The family was sitting at dinner one night, and suddenly Steve announced to us that he'd applied to take the entrance exams for law school.'

'How did your folks react?' asked Karen.

'Dad lit up like a skyrocket. He got so excited he couldn't even eat. He told Steve he'd always prayed that that might happen, that his older son would want to follow in his footsteps. He started talking right then about an eventual partnership. There wasn't a question in anybody's mind, of course, but that Steve would get accepted anywhere he applied. It was just a matter of where he wanted to go.'

'And he decided on the state university?'

'That's where his girlfriend was going. He could probably have got a scholarship to one of the big East Coast colleges if he had wanted one, but he and Susie were pretty tight by then. They were even talking about getting married. He didn't want to go off and leave her.

'So Steve entered law school at the University of New

Mexico, and I dropped out and entered the Police Academy.'

'But – why?' Karen asked in bewilderment. 'If you'd always wanted to be a lawyer, why should Steve's becoming one make any difference?'

'You don't know my brother, or you wouldn't ask that. I've spent my whole life trailing behind him like a second-class also-ran. I knew how he'd do in law school; he'd graduate first in the class. And in practice, he'd be a second Clarence Darrow. And in Dad's law firm—'

'But, why should that affect *you*? I mean, so Steve's brilliant – so he shines at whatever he sets out to do – *so what*? Why should that matter if you really want—'

She broke off her sentence as a plump dark-haired waitress came bustling over to the table.

'How are you this evening?' she asked, flipping open her order book. 'Do you know want you want, or would you like to see a menu?'

'A hamburger and fries, please,' said Ron.

'That's fine with me too.' Karen glanced around the room. 'Is there a phone that I can use? I need to call long distance, but I'll make it collect.'

'There's a pay phone up at the front, next to the postcard rack,' the waitress told her. 'Would you like something to drink with your meal?'

'A Coke,' Ron said, and Karen nodded agreement. He turned to her. 'Are you going to call your folks?'

'I have to,' said Karen. 'In the note I left, I said I'd phone them this evening.'

'What else did you say?'

'That I was going with you to search for the children. Knowing Mom, she probably has the police out looking for me by this time.'

'You're *with* the police,' Ron reminded her.

'That's right, I am. It's hard to think of you that way

when you're not in uniform. I dread making this phone call. My mother is going to be seething.'

'Tell her to cool it,' said Ron. 'The adventure's over. We'll be heading back home as soon as we're done eating.'

Karen slid out of the booth and went to the front of the room where the postcard rack was located. As the waitress had indicated, there was a telephone on a shelf behind it. Karen fed in some dimes, dialled the operator, and gave her name and home phone number.

Her mother must have been waiting next to the telephone, for the receiver was snatched up before the second ring.

'Will you accept a collect call from Karen Connors?' asked the operator.

'Yes, of course,' Mrs Connors said sharply. 'Karen, where are you? Are you all right?'

'I'm fine,' Karen told her. 'We're in Colorado.'

'How could you have done this?' her mother demanded. 'How could you have run off this way the moment my back was turned? Your father and I have been worried out of our minds.'

'You shouldn't have been,' said Karen. 'I left you a note.'

'A note that told us nothing, not where you were going, or why, or what you were planning to do when you got there. Where in Colorado are you?'

'I don't know exactly,' said Karen. 'We're out on the highway somewhere. I think we're short of Colorado Springs by a hundred miles or so. It hardly matters, Mom, because we're coming right back. This was a wild-goose chase.'

'How could you *do* this?' her mother asked again accusingly. 'We had our plans all made. You were in full agreement. You knew I was picking up our tickets and that we were to leave this afternoon.'

'I did know, and I *was* in agreement, but then Ron called. Anne Summers's doctor won't let her take part in the investigation. Ron asked if I'd ride north with him on the Interstate the way Betty and her partner may have done. He thought maybe I'd sense something about the children.'

'And, of course, you told him "yes",' said her mother. 'Just the way you told him "yes" the last time he wanted you to go somewhere with him. What will it take, Karen, for you to start learning from your mistakes? We discussed it all this morning, the problems and the dangers. Do you want to end up like Mrs Summers?'

'That won't happen,' Karen assured her. 'I told you, Mom, we're coming back tonight. You and I can fly to San Francisco tomorrow. What difference does one day make?'

'You really will go? You're not going to back out?'

'We'll go tomorrow, I promise.'

'And you're leaving to drive back now? That means it will be morning before you get here. You're going to be exhausted.'

'I'll sleep in the car,' said Karen.

'Make that young man drive carefully,' said her mother. 'A police officer can have an accident just as easily as anyone else, especially driving at night on mountain roads.'

'I'll see that he's careful,' said Karen. 'Please, Mom, you and Dad stop worrying. Pretend it's Prom night and I'm going to be out till dawn. Go on to bed, and I'll see you in the morning.'

To eliminate further controversy, she quickly hung up the receiver. Glancing over at the booth, she saw that the food had arrived and that Ron had already begun to spread mustard on to his hamburger. As she turned away from the telephone to start across to the table, her shoulder bumped against the postcard rack, and a shower of cards came tumbling out.

'Oh, honestly!' Karen muttered irritably.

She bent to pick up the cards and then stopped suddenly, her right hand suspended six inches above the topmost one. For an unbelieving moment she stood there, frozen. On the floor at her feet, there lay a picture of rose-coloured rock formations. In the background, there towered a snow-capped mountain.

Drawing a shaky breath, Karen forced herself to move again. Hastily, she gathered up the other cards and stuffed them back into the rack.

The card that portrayed the scene from her vision, she carried over to the table.

'Here,' she said quietly, placing it next to Ron's plate. 'Here it is.'

Ron set down the mustard jar and stared at the photograph. 'I don't believe it!' Slowly, he reached for the postcard, lifting it carefully by its edges as though he were afraid that the image might smear with the touch of his fingers. 'Pink rocks, just like you said there'd be. And Anne's mountain. Of course, there would be snow on the top – it's Mount Everest.'

'And the rocks? Do you know what they are?'

'There's bound to be something here to tell us.' He turned the card over and read from the print at the top left corner. ' "The Garden of the Gods is a part of Colorado Springs' city park system. It's noted for its strange rock formations of vivid red sandstone." '

'Colorado Springs!' Karen regarded him breathlessly. 'Can we go there now?'

'We'll get back on the road as soon as we've eaten.'

'I'm too excited to eat,' Karen protested. 'I want to get started.'

'So do I,' Ron said, 'but we're going to have to get some food down. You may not feel hungry, but you're going to need energy. Once the driving is over, my job is done. You're the one who's going to have to find the kids.'

'What if I can't?' Karen asked nervously. 'This afternoon, I didn't sense anything, even the fact that we were on the right road. What if I've lost the ability – or the talent – or whatever it is? What if it never works again?'

'You haven't lost it,' Ron said with certainty. 'You aren't practised yet in controlling it, that's all. As soon as we're back in the car and out on the road again, it's going to come back to you.'

'You sound so sure.' Karen longed to believe him.

'I believe in omens. Your finding this picture was a good one.'

It was the first time since she had met him that Karen could remember seeing him smile.

By the time they had paid for their meal and had left the restaurant, twilight had faded into darkness. The cloudless sky arched high above them, pin-pricked by stars and slashed by a sharp, pale sliver of moon.

When they pulled out on to the highway, Karen knew immediately that Ron had been right. She had not lost the power; it was still there inside her. She could feel its pressure at her temples and behind her eyes. Her head was beginning to throb in a manner that could have been the introduction to a headache, but was, in fact, something quite different. There was no pain involved, only a feeling of increasing tension, and when she closed her eyes, the insides of her lids seemed ready for illumination.

She kept her eyes closed and her mind standing open. Ron rolled down the window beside him, and the sweet night air whipped through the car and filled it with the rich, pine breath of mountain summer. Karen's heart was pounding in rhythm with the car wheels as they drummed the road, and out past the windows she could feel the trees rushing by, and the hills and streams and mountains, and beyond those, houses and people, and the twinkling lights of towns and a distant city.

Time slid past, unpunctuated by conversation.

Up ahead of them, the reality of the sandstone rocks loomed larger. Karen's sense of their existence was growing stronger with each passing mile. Now that she had seen them in a photograph, she did not require a vision to be able to picture them, towering high and jagged, over a valley of coarse, pink sand.

But, the children – *where were the children*? They had been there once; of that she was certain. She did not sense them now, though, and she could not call up their images. No matter how hard she tried to force it open, the third eye remained tightly and stubbornly sealed.

Ron was slowing the car, evidently planning to stop there.

'Ron?' The sound of her voice was jarring after the long silence. 'The kids aren't here, Ron. This isn't where they took them.'

'You must have been dozing,' Ron said as though he hadn't heard her statement. 'We're into the park now.' He pulled the car off the road and brought it to a stop, though he left the engine running. 'You can't see the rocks, but they're here, they're all around us. This *has* to be the place, Karen. The description fits too perfectly for it not to be.'

'It *is* the place in my vision,' agreed Karen. 'They did drive through here with the children. They stopped close to this very spot, and the man got out. The woman slid over into the driver's seat.' For one shining moment she almost thought she had it; though jerky and out of focus, the picture was materializing. 'This is where they changed drivers. The man was angry about the noise the kids were making. He told the woman to do something about it, and she shook her head and told him—'

Abruptly, Karen fell silent.

'She told him what?' Ron prodded.

'It's gone,' Karen said. 'I've lost it.' To her disgust, she found herself blinking back tears.

'You're tired,' Ron said gently. 'You'll get a hold on it in the morning. The thing to do now is to try to get some sleep.'

'Here?' Karen asked. 'Do you mean in the car?'

'We're in a state park,' Ron reminded her. 'This is a

designated camping area. I've got sleeping bags in the car trunk. My friend Chris and I do a lot of impulse camping in the summer.'

He shut off the ignition and got out of the car. Karen heard the sound of the car trunk being opened and slammed shut again. Then Ron came around to the passenger side and opened the door.

'The sky's clear,' he said. 'I don't think we'll have any problem. We'll start driving again in the morning when we're fresher.'

Too worn out to argue, even if she had wanted to, Karen got out of the car and fell into step behind him. When they had walked a short distance, Ron stopped and laid out the sleeping bags.

'Take the bag on the left,' he said. 'That's the one Chris uses. It's a little thicker than this other one.'

'I'm tired enough so I'll never know the difference,' Karen told him.

Once she was settled in the bag, however, she was surprised to find that, despite her weariness, sleep did not come easily. The hard ground was alien to her back. The wind sang strange songs in the darkness, and bushes rustled and twigs snapped, and somewhere off to the right, something small and scurrying dislodged some pebbles and scampered away.

The night sky stretched above her like a sleek purple drop cloth. Pale, strange colours seemed to be moving and shifting beyond it, causing the star holes to flicker with varying degrees of brightness. Staring up into them, Karen felt like a voyeur peeking through a million keyholes to observe the activities in an alien world.

'Karen?' Ron said softly. 'Are you still awake?'

'Yes – sort of.' She rolled over to face him. She could see him only as a blurred mound of darkness.

'You were right about what you said about Steve and me. No matter what he decided to do or be, I should have had enough sense to have stayed in college. Dropping out was the dumbest mistake of my life.'

'You didn't drop out totally,' Karen reminded him. 'You did attend the Police Academy.'

'That was another mistake. I'm not cut out to be a cop. Finding that girl in the river left me shaky for days.'

'Then, why not go back and start over?' Karen asked him.

'Leave the force and go back to college?'

'And then to law school. Do what you planned to do in the first place.'

'That would take years.'

They lay for a while in silence. Then, Ron asked suddenly, 'Are you still going steady with that guy with the Pontiac?'

'No,' Karen said. 'Why?'

'I thought if there wasn't a problem, I might kiss you good night.' When she didn't respond, he raised himself up on his elbow and leaned across the space between the sleeping bags. His lips brushed her cheek. 'Good night, sweet kid.'

'Good night,' Karen whispered.

'Is Chris's sleeping bag comfortable?'

'Yes, it's fine.' She paused. 'You didn't mention – is Chris a guy or a girl?'

'He's Christopher Summers, Anne's son. We've been friends since grade school.' From the tone of his voice, she thought that he might be smiling again.

She saw a movement, a pale moth in the darkness, fluttering across to light beside her. When Ron's hand closed around hers, however, she knew that she had been mistaken. There was nothing fragile about the strong, warm grasp.

The night arched above them, no longer a drop cloth, but a canopy studded with diamonds. Holding fast to Ron's hand, Karen let her eyes fall closed. In the final instant before sleep overtook her, she realized, with a feeling that was a blend of fear and exaltation, that, at some point during the past two dreadful days, she had begun to fall in love.

18

Karen woke when the first rays of sunlight touched her eyelids, and, on waking, she knew that the children would be found that day.

There was no reasoning behind this knowledge, it was simply there, as though it had slipped into her consciousness while she lay sleeping. She could feel the children's presence not too far from her. They were so real, so immediate, that she could almost see their faces. For an instant she could have sworn that she could smell warm milk and talcum powder, and that the echo in her ears was the sound of Matthew Wilson's laughter.

Then she registered that the sound had been a bird call.

Opening her eyes, she found herself confronted with a scene that was unlike anything she could ever have imagined. She was lying in the midst of a dazzling fairytale world composed of giant spires with sculptured bases, all glinting an impossible shade of salmon in the stinging brilliance of the glittering morning light. Behind these rocks there glowed a sky that was the same vivid, incredible blue as Ron Wilson's eyes.

Ron, himself, lay sleeping soundly an arm's length away from her. His lips were slightly parted, and he was breathing through his mouth with a soft, whistling sound. The slanted morning sunlight accentuated the clean, strong line of his jaw and the high cheekbones with the shadowy hollows beneath them. A stubble of blond beard had materialized during the night and contrasted oddly with the vulnerable boyishness of his face.

Karen rolled over on to her side to watch him sleeping. How could she ever have failed to realize that he was handsome? She tried to remember the first impression that she had had of him. All she could recall of that initial meeting at the Zenners' was the police uniform and the well-gnawed fingernails and the feeling that he was too young to be doing what he was doing.

Now, as though in response to the intensity of her scrutiny, Ron stirred, stretched and shifted his position. He brought his right hand up and tucked it under his cheek. Karen wondered at what point in the night their hands had parted. Had he consciously let go to turn away from her, or had he fallen asleep, as she had, with his hand in hers?

She said, 'Ron?' Speaking his name in this mystical setting, at this unfamiliar hour, gave her a heady feeling, as though she was sipping champagne for breakfast. 'Ron – it's morning. It's time to wake up.'

He opened his eyes. For a moment he lay, unmoving, gazing blankly up into the great, blue bowl of sky. Then, he seemed to register where he was and who it was that was with him.

'Well, hi, kid,' he said softly, turning his head to look across at Karen. 'How did you sleep? Did the great outdoors really make all that bad a bedroom?'

'Not at all,' Karen said. 'I slept hard, and it's just as you said, I do have a grip on things now. I've got a sense of the children. I can't say where they are exactly, but I *feel* them. I know they're near us, and I think I can find them. No, I don't just think it – I *know* it. We *are* going to find them.'

'That's the news I've been waiting for!' Ron said excitedly.

It took only minutes to roll up the sleeping bags and load them back into the car trunk. There was no sign of life to be seen in any direction. The quiet of the camping ground was so all-encompassing that it was almost as though they were situated on another planet. When Ron started the car to pull out on to the highway, the roar of the engine could have been that of a spacecraft, taking off from the desert surface of an alien world.

Several miles down the road they pulled into a combination service station and coffee shop to pick up take-out food for breakfast and to buy gas.

While Ron was filling the gas tank, Karen went inside to use the rest room. Once there, she gave her hands and face a much needed scrubbing and attacked her tangled hair with a pocket comb. Her mouth still held the taste of the hamburger she had eaten the previous night, and she wished she had thought to slip a toothbrush into her purse before she had left the house.

At that point, of course, she had not known that she would be gone for more than one day. If she had, she would have brought a change of clothing with her also. Her suitcase had been partially packed in readiness for the trip to San Francisco. It would have been a simple thing to have closed it and brought it with her.

Abandoning the wishful thinking, she did the best job she could at smoothing the wrinkles out of her blouse and dusting the coarse red sand off her jeans. When she re-entered the coffee shop, she found Ron there, waiting for her, with a Styrofoam cup in each of his hands and a package of sweet rolls tucked under one arm.

'There's a phone booth out in front,' he told her. 'While we're here, don't you think you ought to call your parents?'

'I ought to, yes,' said Karen. 'I don't know, though, if I can face it. By this time, my mother will be ready to kill me.'

'Probably,' Ron agreed. 'When you explain to her, though, about that postcard, she's bound to understand.'

'Explain to my *mother*?' Karen said incredulously. 'You've met her, Ron. You know what she's like. Nobody ever "explains" anything to Mom. She was furious enough that I came up here in the first place. When I tell her that we haven't even left yet to drive back, she's going to hit the ceiling.'

'You have to call her,' Ron said reasonably. 'You told

her she could expect you home this morning. If you don't check in, she'll think we've been in a wreck.'

Karen sighed and nodded.

'I know you're right,' she agreed reluctantly. 'OK, I'll make the call, but don't be surprised if you see flames shooting out of the receiver. Mom's probably sitting there next to the telephone, waiting with a flamethrower.'

To her surprise, however, when she did make the call, the voice that answered was not her mother's, but her father's.

'Where are you?' he demanded. 'We've been worried to death. We expected you home hours ago. What's happened?'

'Everything's fine,' Karen told him. 'There've been some new developments, that's all. We've decided to keep on driving for a little while longer.'

'Do you mean to say that you're still in Colorado?' Her father's voice was sharp with irritation. 'You haven't even started back yet? Where on earth did you sleep last night?'

'At the Garden of the Gods,' Karen told him. 'We're in a state park. Ron had brought along sleeping bags, and we slept out in the open on the ground.'

'Well, I want you to get yourself back here, and I mean *pronto*!' said Mr Connors. 'If Officer Wilson refuses to drive you, then take a bus. Do you have money? If you don't, I'll wire your bus fare. We want you home, Karen. We're very worried.'

'I can't come home just yet, Dad,' Karen tried to explain to him. 'I was starting to tell you, I think I can find the children. I have this feeling they're somewhere right up ahead of us. If we drive just a little way further—'

'Karen, I've *had* it with this sort of thing!' her father exploded. 'This whole business is getting more and more ridiculous! I don't want to hear any more about these crazy premonitions. Running off the way you did was cruel and irresponsible. Your mother has been worried sick about you. You know she can't take pressure like this. She's in bed right now with a head-splitting migraine.'

'Please, tell her to stop worrying,' said Karen. 'There's nothing for either one of you to be upset about. Ron and I are together, and he's looking out for me. He's a police officer, for heaven's sake! He's trained to take care of people. Everything here is fine, and we *are* going to find those kids. Believe it or not, as you like, Dad, but we are.'

Before her father could respond, she said hastily, 'I'll call you this evening. That is, I will if I'm not home by then, which I might be. Goodbye, and, please, stop worrying about me.'

She hung up the receiver and stepped out of the phone booth back into the sparkling brilliance of the Colorado morning.

Ron was sitting in his car in front of the coffee shop, munching on sweet rolls and washing them down with coffee. When he saw her emerge from the booth, he gave the car horn a beep.

Karen hurriedly crossed the parking lot and climbed in beside him.

'Well, that's done, thank goodness,' she said with relief. She picked up the coffee cup that he had set out for her on the dashboard and took a grateful gulp of the hot black liquid. 'I could have used this reinforcement *before* making that phone call.'

'I didn't see any sparks fly,' said Ron, extending the package of rolls so she could take one. 'Was it as bad as you expected?'

'Not quite,' Karen told him. 'Luckily, it was Dad who answered and not my mother. He's mad enough, but Mom must be even worse. Dad says she's collapsed with a migraine.'

'You don't sound too sympathetic,' Ron commented.

'I would be, except I'm too used to having her do that. Mom always gets headaches when things don't go her way.'

She took a roll from the package, bit into it, and chewed on it thoughtfully. 'You know, of course, that Mom and I don't get along very well. Despite that, though, my mother's the one who believes me. I've never understood that – why my mother should accept the fact that I'm a psychic, when my father doesn't.'

Ron turned the key in the ignition and started the engine.

'Maybe your dad doesn't want to believe it and your mother does.'

'No, that's not how it is. Mom hates my being "different". She wants me to hide it and not let anyone know. She's always wished that she had a "normal" daughter, as well adjusted and popular as she was when she was a teenager. To hear Mom talk, she was right in the middle of everything – on the cheerleading squad, Homecoming Queen, sorority girl.'

'That doesn't sound much like the type of person who gets migraines. I thought they were stress-related.'

'I don't know what causes them, really. I just know she gets them.' Karen leaned back in her seat. 'Are we ready to get started?'

'I guess we're as ready as we'll ever be. Do you know where we're headed?'

'Just keep driving north, the way we've been going,' Karen told him. 'I'm pretty sure that I'll know when we come to the turnoff.'

They drove for over an hour without much talking, watching the lush mountain scenery roll past the car windows on either side of them. Karen finished her sweet roll and then ate a second. She kept her mind directed towards the children. Every so often she closed her eyes and attempted to call up a vision of what they were doing. On one occasion, she found that she could see light and movement, but the scene that leapt and wavered upon her mind's dark screen would not come into focus.

As time passed, however, she began to experience a

steadily growing sense of physical nearness to the house by the river that Anne had described to them. With every mile they travelled, she felt them drawing closer. When Ron broke the silence to say, 'We're on the outskirts of Denver,' she immediately responded, 'That's not where we want to go. There should be a side road coming up soon on the left. We want to take that.'

Ron nodded, accepting the statement. When, after they had driven another mile or so, the side road did appear, he slowed the car without comment and turned off the smooth asphalt highway on to a narrow pitted lane that ran off to the west.

Now the driving became more difficult and their pace much slower. The road curved and wandered as though uncertain of its own destination, meandering first along the fringes of a pine forest, then jutting back and forth in a series of wild S-turns to avoid a family of boulders, then twisting to take a sudden, startling plunge into a gorge to cross a bridge above a narrow river.

At the sight of the surging water, Karen's feeling of well-being abruptly vanished. The memory of that other river – of Carla's terrible river – came rushing back to her, and she saw once again the images from her dream – tiny bodies in diapers and nightgowns being tossed about like foam. Her stomach lurched, and the acid taste of the coffee she had consumed several hours earlier rose in her throat until it threatened to gag her.

Glancing sideways at Ron, she saw that he, too, was reacting to the similarity of the circumstances. His jaw was set, and his face showed pale beneath the shadow of morning beard.

'This is different,' he said, without attempting to elaborate.

Silently, Karen nodded. The situation was different, and so was the road they were travelling. This road did not dead-end at the river as the other had done; instead, it turned to run parallel, tuning itself to the curves and twists of the bank to form a border for the singing green water.

'Are you sure this is right?' Ron asked at last. 'Could there have been another road up ahead that we should have waited for? We haven't seen a sign of life since we turned off the highway. We haven't even passed a car going in the other direction.'

'This is right,' Karen said. 'I know it.'

And, as she spoke the words, the picture was *there*. It came so suddenly and with such total clarity that it blocked her view of the road ahead of them. With a gasp of surprise, she found herself staring into what appeared to be a make-shift nursery. The room was filled with cribs, in many of which there lay sleeping infants. The side was down on one of the cribs, and a woman bent over it, engaged in the process of dressing one of the children. Although the figure of the woman obscured her sight of the baby, Karen knew instinctively that the child was Matthew.

He was awake and thrashing; she could tell that by the woman's jerky movements as she struggled to work his arms into the sleeves of a T-shirt. The other children seemed unnaturally quiet for this time of morning, lying limp and placid in their beds, with only an occasional involuntary twitch of arm or leg muscles to show that they were not dolls on display in a toy store.

'They've been tranquillized,' said Karen.

'What did you say?' Ron asked, startled.

'The children have been tranquillized,' Karen repeated. 'They haven't been hurt, but Betty has given them something to keep them sleeping. All except Matthew. He was sleeping earlier, but whatever they gave him has been allowed to wear off now. Betty is dressing him. She's going to take him someplace.'

'How do you know that?' Ron asked hoarsely. 'What is it you see?'

'There's a room, a sort of an office.' For an instant it

was there before her, superimposed like a ghost image upon the vision of the nursery. 'It's small. There's nothing there except some chairs and a desk with a telephone. It's in the city, I think; I can hear the sound of traffic. They don't keep their files there. They use it only as a meeting place.'

'Their files?'

'The files in which they keep their business records are out at the house. It's a good-sized house, though it's only one storey. There's a long living room with windows looking out on the river. There's a kitchen and there are several bedrooms. The children are in a big one in the back. The walls inside are natural wood. The outside's made of raw logs, like a hunting cabin. I can see—'

She broke off her description, for it was no longer necessary. As they took the next curve in the road, they *both* could see the house, back at the edge of the woods, on the far side of the river.

They could also see, at the side of it, half hidden by trees, the back end of a blue van.

19

Ron's hands tightened on the wheel until the knuckles grew white, but he did not reduce the speed at which he was driving until the house had been passed and lost to view around the next curve. Then he pressed his foot to the brake and pulled the car over to the side of the road, bringing it to an abrupt halt on a flat, grassy patch of ground next to the river.

He shut off the engine and sat without speaking. He seemed to be trying to decide what to do.

It was Karen who broke the silence.

'How do you suppose they were able to get the van to that side of the river?'

'There must be a back road,' Ron said. 'Come to think of it, I think I remember seeing a trail of some kind leading off to the left before we crossed the bridge. You didn't tell me to turn there.'

'I missed it,' Karen admitted. 'I didn't expect it to be there.'

'Well, you didn't miss *much*,' Ron said. 'You got that house pegged perfectly. It looks just like you said it would. If you tell me the kids are in there, I'll take your word for it. And the office you were talking about – the one in the city – of course, they must have to have that. They need a separate place to meet with the couples.'

'What do you mean?' Karen asked. 'What couples?'

'It explains why they didn't ask ransom,' said Ron. 'They've never had any intention of returning those kids. Haven't you figured it out yet? They're running an adoption agency. They're selling black-market babies and probably racking up a fortune.'

'They're selling *babies*!' Karen repeated. 'Who buys

them? Any couple that wants a baby and can't have one can go to an adoption agency.'

'And be put on a mile-long waiting list,' said Ron. 'From what I've heard, the wait can take over five years. Even then, there's no guarantee a kid will be available. Here in the Southwest especially, there are a lot more people wanting healthy, light-skinned babies than there are kids like that to go around.'

'But on television they have that programme called "Wednesday's Child",' protested Karen. 'They *advertise* to get parents for orphaned children.'

'Well, sure, but those aren't cute little babies they're talking about. They're older kids and handicapped kids and kids of mixed races. Most people don't want those. They want babies like Matt.'

'Gerber babies,' Karen said softly, recalling how she had used that term less than a week before. 'Perfect children.'

'Yeah, perfect children. They're worth a bundle, especially when they're infants. Half-grown children come equipped with problems. Why take a shopworn specimen if you can buy unused merchandise?'

'That's terrible!' breathed Karen. 'Babies aren't "merchandise"!'

'To these people they are. To them, this is a business, and Matt must be their blue ribbon special. You said you saw Betty getting him dressed to take out somewhere. I'd be willing to bet he's not expected back.'

Karen nodded. What he said made sense.

'What can we do?'

'I wish I knew how to play it,' Ron continued. 'The way I see it, we've got two choices. One is to go back the way we came and contact the state police. I could try to talk them into sending armed men out here with a search warrant. I'm afraid, though, that they wouldn't do it.'

'Why?' Karen asked in surprise. 'You're a police officer

yourself. If you told them the children were out here, wouldn't they believe you?'

'I'm a rookie cop from out of state,' Ron said, 'I've got no authority of any kind here in Colorado. And, what do I tell them, anyway? "I've got a girlfriend out in the car who has these weird sort of visions. Her vibes tell her there are kidnapped babies in a house stuck off in the mountains." I can picture the reaction. They'll think I've flipped out.'

'They could call the police back in Albuquerque for verification.'

'Verification of *what*? They don't even know I'm up here.'

'They don't even *know*!' Karen exclaimed. 'You mean, you brought me up here—'

'Completely on my own, against all orders. I'm off the case, remember? The truth of it is, when I get back, I'll probably also find myself off the force.'

'So, what do you see as our other choice?' Karen asked him.

'It would help if we went in there with something solid to offer. If I could report that I'd actually seen those kids, they'd be more inclined to listen.' He studied the river appraisingly. 'The water's running fast, but it doesn't look as though it's very deep. There shouldn't be any problem getting across here. That line of flat rocks makes a natural bridge.'

'The room they're using as a nursery is at the back of the house,' said Karen. 'The trees are so thick there that I think we could get a look through the window without running much risk of being spotted.'

'There's no "we" about it,' Ron said. 'I'm doing this alone.'

'No you're not,' said Karen. 'We're in this together. I'm coming too.'

'Karen, please don't give me a hard time about this,'

Ron said tersely. 'I said, you're not coming, and I meant it. Just accept that, will you? We don't have time to argue.'

He leaned across and pressed the button on the front of the glove compartment. The door fell open, and he reached into the compartment's interior and drew out a pistol in a holster. Karen watched in silence as he strapped on the belt and settled the holster against his right hip. She was stunned to realize that the weapon had been lying there, less than an arm's length away from her, during the entire drive up from Albuquerque.

'Could you use that?' she asked.

'Sure, I can use it. What do you think they taught us at the Academy?'

'I didn't ask "*Can* you?", I asked, "*Could* you?" Do you think you could shoot somebody?'

'I don't know,' Ron said. 'I hope that I could if I had to.' He changed subject abruptly. 'Do you drive?'

'I have my licence. I'm not very experienced.'

'I'm going to leave the keys in the ignition. I want you to stay right here and keep the doors locked. If I'm not back in half an hour, drive back to the highway. Locate a telephone and call the State Police.'

Karen said, 'For God's sake, be careful!'

'I will be, and you be too. If anything happens – if you hear a shot or see somebody coming towards the car – start the engine and get yourself out of here. Don't stop to think about anything, just hit the accelerator.'

He pulled her towards him and kissed her. This time it was no little peck on the cheek. His mouth came down firmly upon hers, and his arms closed tight around her. When he lifted his face at last, she thought she might drown in the blue of his eyes.

'What you suggested last night, about my going back to college,' Ron said softly. 'I've decided to do it. So what if it takes four more years? The end result will be worth it. I'll be doing what I want to do.'

Karen pressed her face against his shoulder.

'Ron, I'm scared,' she whispered. 'I have this feeling.'

'Another vision?'

'No, just a feeling. These people are dangerous. Look what they did to Anne!'

'I won't take dumb chances,' Ron assured her. 'All I'm going to do is take one quick look and come back to the car. Believe me, kid, I'm no storybook hero. I'm not going into that place without backup.'

He gave her a quick, hard hug, opened the door and got out of the car. Karen reached over and pulled the door shut again. She pushed down the lock and sat, watching, as Ron strode down the slanted bank to the edge of the river. As he had commented, the water was running fast, but not high, and the line of flat-topped rocks that stood exposed above its surface formed a natural bridge to the opposite bank.

He stepped on to the first of these, found his balance, and moved out on to the next one. Within minutes he had completed the trip across the river and was standing on the far side. He turned to glance back at the car. Then, lifting his hand in a reassuring salute, he turned and disappeared into a thicket of pine trees.

Settling back in her seat, Karen tried to force herself to relax. The clock on the dashboard read eleven twenty-seven. Another half hour would bring it to almost noon. The next thirty minutes loomed before her as endless as all eternity. If everything went as smoothly as Ron anticipated, how could it possibly take him an entire half hour to slip up to the house, peer through the window, and return? Surely, in twenty minutes at the most, he would be back again. If he wasn't, she didn't know if she could bear it.

In an attempt to calm herself, she turned her eyes to the bounding river as it twinkled and sparkled beneath the brilliance of the overhead sun. Along its shallow edges, pale, thin-washed stones gleamed up through the crystal water, and the surface was dappled with pagan coins of golden light. At its centre, the river ran green as emeralds except at those spots at which it swirled around rocks and broke into flying spittles of snowy foam.

Despite the heat of midday and the stuffiness of the closed car, Karen found herself shivering. She knew how unreasonable it was to hate all rivers because of one cruel experience, but the reaction was something over which she had no control. Perhaps, a time would come when she would be able to view such a sight with pleasure, but it did not seem likely that this would occur very soon.

Hypnotized by the dancing light, she lowered the lids of her outer eyes in an attempt to focus her inner one upon Ron. To her surprise, she was able to find him immediately. He had left the thicket by the river and was working his way around the edge of a flower-studded clearing. Although he was now very close to the house, he was still separated from it by a narrow strip of woods which served as a shield against the eyes of its inhabitants. He was moving slowly and carefully, but with an air of self-confidence. The black butt of the police revolver protruded from the holster at his hip.

Concentrating upon his progress along the outskirts of the tiny meadow, Karen began to experience the acute sense of smell that always accompanied such visions. She caught the fragrance of purple clover and wild flowers far more intensely than if she had been standing in the field among them. Drawing a deep mental breath, she inhaled the pungent perfume of the pine needles that formed the carpet beneath Ron's feet. Although the windows of the car were rolled high, she could smell the damp breeze that blew up from the river to ruffle his hair and the rich, dark aroma of wet leaves and water-soaked earth.

And – *something else*. An alien odour that should not have been there. Something not part of the woods that encircled them or of the people in the house beyond the trees.

Leaving Ron to continue moving forward at his own pace, Karen sent her mind flying on ahead of him with the third eye wide open and alert for possible danger. The nearer she drew to the house, the stronger the odour became. It was the heated smell of something alive. Hair. Saliva. Warm, rancid breath. The stench of animal droppings. The fetid odour of raw meat, half spoiled from prolonged exposure to the summer sun.

Quite suddenly, she recognized the source of the odours. Somewhere, close by, there was a *dog*.

Almost as soon as she became aware of its existence, her third eye caught sight of it, lying in the shade of some bushes at the back of the house. It was a Doberman, huge and well muscled, and clearly functioning as a guard dog. It was wearing a collar, and Karen's initial impression was that it might be chained. Then, it lifted its head, and she saw that there was nothing restraining it. It had evidently chosen to settle where it had, not because it had been confined there, but to escape the heat of the sun. A dish of meat scraps had been set on the ground outside the kitchen door, and it was this that was contributing the stench of decay to the repertoire of offensive odours that was assailing her.

The shock of seeing the massive animal was enough to bring her physical eyes snapping open. She was back in the car by the river, and her mouth was dry with horror. She had seen Ron's response to the harmless, yapping puppy at the Sanchez house. What would his reaction be when he was faced with the vicious-looking creature that now lay in wait only a matter of yards ahead?

The dog that had attacked him in childhood had been a Doberman. To be faced with this current monster would have to be the incarnation of every night terror he had ever experienced. It was true, he was wearing a pistol, but what if the shock of the unexpected confrontation kept him from reacting quickly enough? If he did fire the gun, the sound of the shot would give away his presence to the inhabitants of the house. What would happen then?

There was no other answer; she had to reach and warn him. Throwing open the door, Karen hastily scrambled out of the car and hurried down the sloping bank to the edge of the river. There was no way to cross it except by the rocks that Ron had utilized. Much as she hated the prospect, she would have to use them as well.

Determinedly closing off her mind to the existence of the rushing water, she decided to confront each step as a separate challenge. Only after clearing one rock would she look ahead to the next one. Progressing in this manner, she found the expedition less hazardous than she had anticipated. Luckily, the rocks were all comparatively flat-surfaced and broad enough to allow her ample footspace. Her worst moment was when she reached the river's centre point and discovered that the next stone was half again as far from its predecessor as the others. Bracing herself, she extended her right leg as far as possible and gave a hard, quick shove with her home-based left foot. The right foot settled securely upon its landing place, and she transferred her full weight on to it with a gasp of relief.

Once she had completed the crossing, she plunged recklessly into the thicket, more intent upon making speed than exercising caution. Dried sticks and crisp pine cones crackled beneath her hurrying feet, and small twigs snapped as she roughly shoved them aside to create a pathway. In only a matter of minutes she had reached the clearing that had been the focal point of her last vision. It was just as she had seen it in her mind, a miniature meadow sprinkled with wild flowers and separated from the house beyond it by a thin screen of woods.

She peered hopefully about in search of Ron, but could see him nowhere. By now, of course, he was probably in among the trees. Was there a chance, she wondered frantically, that she could still catch up with him? She longed to call out his name, but she knew that the dog had keener ears than he did. The last thing she wanted was to alert it that strangers were approaching.

It was a moment before the realisation struck her that she was not alone. The child had been standing so quietly at the far side of the clearing that she might have been an especially tall flower on a slender stalk, silhouetted against the green of the summer-dark trees.

Karen stared at her, incredulous.

'It's you again! Why are *you* here? What is it you want?'

The little girl's head was bent, so her face was lost in shadow, but the fine, pale hair shimmered in the sunlight. She looked so small, so fragile, and in some strange way so achingly familiar, that Karen felt an overwhelming longing to gather her into her arms.

The child's own arms were extended with the palms of her hands turned outward in a gesture that was more eloquent than words.

Stop! Please, stop! Don't go any farther! Escape while you can!

'I can't do that,' Karen told her softly. 'Ron's life is in danger.'

'*So is mine!*'

It was the first time that she had heard the girl's actual voice, but, despite this fact, it, too, was familiar. It was pure and sweet as the chirp of a bird.

'*Stop!*' the child cried again. And she called Karen by a name that no one had called her by before.

'What do you mean?' Karen was stunned by what she had heard. 'Why did you call me that? You're not – you *can't* be—'

It was then that she heard the growl. It was followed by a moment of such absolute silence that she had one fleeting instant of hope that she had been mistaken about the source of the sound. Then, pure chaos erupted. There was a ferocious snarl and the sound of a screen door crashing open. A man's voice shouted, and then a woman's. As an accompaniment to their voices, there came a volley of ferocious barking.

It was too late! She had delayed too long!

'Ron!' Karen breathed. 'Oh, dear God, *Ron!*'

There were two gunshots in quick succession, and all ability to reason vanished.

Instead of racing for the car, she did the worst thing possible.

She screamed.

20

At first, she didn't tie the sounds to herself. She heard them in bewilderment, uncertain as to where they were coming from. It was only after several moments had passed that she realised incredulously that those piercing shrieks were hers. They were originating from somewhere deep inside her and seemed to be surging up through her throat of their own volition.

The man who emerged from the clump of trees put an immediate end to them. The sight of the gun in his hand extinguished her hysterics and brought Karen back into control of herself as abruptly as though she had been doused with ice water. She pressed her hands to her mouth, choking back any last shreds of sound, and stared in hatred at the well-remembered face.

It seemed to take Jed a moment to recognise her. Once he did, it was evident from his expression that she was the last person he had expected to find there.

'Well,' he said, 'so it's our little friend from Albuquerque.'

The sound of his voice brought back the feel of the crushing hand across her mouth and the salty taste of her own blood. Her stomach lurched, and she fought back a rising tide of nausea.

'What have you done to Ron?' she whispered.

'If "Ron" is the guy who just killed my dog, he's got a bullet in him.'

Karen's legs went weak beneath her.

'Is he – is he still—' She couldn't bring forth the words. She was too terrified of how the question would be answered.

'He's alive,' Jed said. He gestured with the pistol. 'Turn around and start walking. Take that path between those trees over there. I'm going to be right behind you, so don't try anything funny. Where'd you leave your car?'

'Across the river,' Karen told him.

'That explains, then, why we didn't hear the engine. Who else is with you?'

'Nobody.'

'Just you and the boyfriend?'

'Yes, just the two of us.'

The instant she spoke, she wished that she could snatch back the statement. In the shock and confusion of the moment, she had told him too much and had made herself and Ron appear too obviously defenceless. How much better it would have been if she could somehow have managed to present the impression that they had backup help available!

But, the moment for that was over; because of her stupidity, they now had no bartering power of any kind. Reluctantly, she obeyed the command and moved towards the trees. Although she did not turn her head to look back, she could sense the man's presence so close behind her that she expected at any moment to feel the pressure of the gun against the small of her back.

The footpath had not been visible from across the clearing, but when they reached the trees it seemed to unroll magically before them. After a matter of several yards, they broke through the strip of woods, and Karen found herself facing the back wall of the house that she and Ron had viewed earlier from the far side of the river.

The scene that now confronted her told its own story. The body of a large black dog lay stretched full-length on the ground. Its legs were extended both before and behind it as though it had been rendered lifeless in mid-leap. The largest part of its head had been blown away, and the portion that remained resembled the pulp of a spattered melon, seeded with fragments of splintered white bone.

The woman, Betty, was holding Ron's gun. Ron,

himself, sat doubled over on the wooden steps, his left hand clutching at his right shoulder. Blood flowed from between his fingers, and the sleeve that he was gripping was red and soaking.

Karen gasped, too horrified to speak.

Ron lifted his head. His face was ashen.

'I told you to get yourself out of here,' he said.

'It was the dog.' Karen brought out the words with difficulty. 'I wanted to warn you about the dog.'

'That was crazy,' Ron said. 'You could have got away. Now, you've blown it – we've both of us blown it.'

Betty was regarding Karen with icy eyes.

'It's a surprise seeing you here, I must say. We read in the paper about the Great Smoke Alarm Escape. Why didn't you rest on your laurels and quit while you were ahead?' She glanced questioningly at Jed. 'Is there anyone with them?'

'I'm pretty sure not,' the man said. 'The girl says their car's parked over on the road. They must have come across on the rocks. You should have let me finish the job on her back at the apartment.'

'It didn't seem necessary,' said Betty. 'I never imagined—'

'That's the trouble with you – you "never imagine" there could ever be problems. You never think anything could possibly go wrong with any plan you come up with. Well, this time I'm the one who'll make the decisions.' He gave Karen a sharp poke with the muzzle of the pistol. 'I want you up those steps and into that house. You – Boyfriend – whoever the hell you are – get up and get in there with her.'

'But he's hurt!' objected Karen. 'Look how he's bleeding!'

'He can walk and bleed at the same time. Come on – get inside, both of you!'

This is a dream, Karen told herself. It's all just a nightmare.

There had been so many dreams, waking ones, sleeping ones – flowing one into another in such bewildering succession – how could she be sure whether any one experience was or wasn't real? In a moment or so, perhaps, she would awaken. She would find herself at home in her own bedroom with the leaves of the backyard elm tree fluttering at the window and bird voices chirping and sunlight falling in patterns across the blue carpet. Or, better yet, she would be stretched in a sleeping bag in a wild, red wonderland, and Ron would be lying across from her, smiling in his sleep.

Unless and until that happened, however, she had to accept the situation as she now perceived it. Moving like a robot, she crossed to the back steps. She passed so close to the body of the dog that she felt the bristle of its hair brush against her ankle. Flies had already begun to gather, their monotonous hum growing increasingly louder with an underlying, vicious, buzz-saw intensity.

Karen didn't look down. She didn't look at Ron as she moved past him. She had a vague impression that Betty was now beside him, preparing to haul him to his feet.

That won't hurt him. Not if this is a dream. Soon I'll be waking. Soon it will be over.

She ascended the steps and went in through a door that led into a tiny, foul-smelling kitchen. Glass jars of commercially prepared baby food and an assortment of empty beer cans littered the counter next to the stove top, and the sink was piled with crusted dishes and nursing bottles filled to various levels with souring milk.

Karen paused uncertainly. What was she supposed to do now? she wondered. As though in response to the unvoiced question, she received another brisk jab with the handgun. Obediently, she continued on across the kitchen and through a second door into the front room of the house. It was furnished with an overstuffed sofa, unmatched chairs, and a wooden picnic table on which there sat a portable typewriter and a small metal filing cabinet. Two narrow windows on the north wall faced out upon the river.

In the room's far corner, there stood a playpen, and in it, dressed neatly in bright red rompers and a striped T-shirt, sat Matthew Wilson.

The little boy glanced up from a pile of plastic building blocks to stare at Karen. His round face was solemn, as if he were pondering whether or not he knew her. Then his eyes moved beyond her, and he let out a crow of happy recognition. Grabbing for the side bars, he began a frantic scramble to hoist himself up into a standing position.

Karen turned to see Ron behind her, standing in the doorway. He was leaning against the door frame as if he needed it for support. At the sudden sight of his nephew, he pulled himself upright and took an impetuous step towards him. Then, reeling, he released his hold on his own shoulder and made a grab for the edge of the table.

Karen's manufactured lassitude abruptly vanished. She could no longer hide from reality. This was not a dream, no matter how much she might wish that it were. It was real, horribly real. Ron was badly injured.

She moved quickly to his side.

'We've got to stop the bleeding!'

Jed addressed himself to Ron as though she had not spoken.

'Get over there on the sofa. I've got some questions.' He gestured towards Karen. 'Help him get over there before he falls over.'

'I'm dizzy,' Ron muttered.

'Lean on me,' Karen said. 'It'll be all right. You're going to be OK.'

She spoke the words with as much conviction as she could muster, but she could not make herself believe them.

There was nothing 'OK' about any part of what was happening.

With her arm around his waist and with his left arm draped across her shoulders, she managed somehow to propel them both across to the sofa. Easing Ron down on to it, she glanced hastily about for something that could be used for a tourniquet.

'Where are the clean diapers?' she asked imperatively. 'We can use them for bandages!'

Ignoring the question, Betty stared past her, out through the dirty pane of the nearest of the windows.

'I don't see their car. I thought it was supposed to be parked over there on the road.'

'It's around the bend,' Karen told her. She fought to keep the thin edge of her panic from surfacing in her voice. 'Please, do something. We can't let him keep on losing blood this way.'

'Which one of you has the keys?' Jed asked her.

'They're still in the ignition.'

'We'd better get the car moved,' said Betty. 'If somebody comes looking for these two, it will be as good as a signpost.'

'That can wait a few minutes,' Jed said. 'First, I want to find out about something.' Ron had by this time so obviously passed the stage for possible interrogation, that, by default, he was forced to direct the question towards Karen. 'How did you find us? How did you know we were up here?'

In the silence that followed, Karen could hear the thud of her own racing heartbeat. What answer could she come up with that these people would believe? To tell them the truth would be suicidal. It was doubtful that they would accept it, and, if they did, it would brand her as a threat. If she could mentally track them now from one state to another, what would there be to stop her from doing future tracking? As long as she existed, they would never be safe from detection. No matter where in the country they might choose to relocate, she would always be able to find them.

Betty spoke up suddenly.

'That Summers woman told them. I warned you about her back in Dallas. I knew she was going to be bad news.'

'It wasn't her,' said Jed. 'If it was, the law would be up here. That lady's got clout. When she talks, cops listen. No, it's the girl who got on to us somehow. She came up looking for us and brought along the boyfriend. You must have let something drop when you were with her in the car.'

'I let nothing "drop",' Betty said curtly. 'There's something strange going on here. It's like with Anne Summers, when she told reporters that I was a natural redhead and you had a beard. She'd never seen us, but she could describe us.'

'That woman was a psychic. We both of us read that piece about her in the paper.'

'Maybe Karen's one too. Has that ever occurred to you?'

'You're nuts,' said Jed. 'She's a kid.'

'So, what does that prove? Everybody starts out as "a kid". Anne Summers was a kid once.' Betty consulted her watch. 'I've got to get a move on. I'm due in the city with the baby in less than an hour. We'll be getting a good price for this one. The couple's old and rolling in money. I bet they're good for at least fifty thousand.'

'Then go,' said Jed. 'I'll take care of things here.'

'First, I want that car moved.'

'So move it! Who's stopping you?'

'*You* move it,' said Betty. 'I'm not going to jump stones across that creek. *I'll* keep tabs on our friends.'

'There's only one who needs watching.' Jed nodded toward Karen. 'As for that guy there—'

Ron had slumped over into the corner of the sofa. His eyes were closed and his face was the colour of chalk.

With no real notion of how one detected vital signs,

Karen grabbed his left wrist and frantically groped for a pulse beat.

'Let him be,' Jed commanded.

'*Let him be?*' She regarded him incredulously. 'Let him *be*, when he may be *dying*? Please, can't either of you do *something*! If you'll take him to a doctor, I'll tell you anything you want to know!'

What was it that Jed had asked her? Was it how she had known where to find them?

'Betty was right,' Karen said in a rush. 'I *am* like Anne Summers. I knew where you were because I could see this place in my mind. The mountain – the road – the river – I could see all of them. I could see this house – the babies – Matthew – I could see Betty dressing him. I knew he was wearing red before we ever got here. I saw the dog; that's why I left the car. I was trying to get to Ron before he walked straight into it.'

She had lost all control of what her voice was saying. Words came tumbling out of her mouth in a babbling torrent. She was not aware that she was crying until she felt the heat of tears on her cheeks and heard the ugly, rasping sound of her own harsh sobbing.

'What else can I tell you? I'll tell you everything – everything! I know about the office you have in Denver. That's where you meet with people to sell them babies. There are files on all the adoptions in that box over there. Except for Matthew, the children here now are in the back bedroom. You've doped them with something to keep them quiet and sleeping.'

What did it matter what she told them? What did anything matter? It had been insane of her to have dreamed that there might be hope for them. Neither she nor Ron would be leaving this house alive.

Dropping Ron's limp wrist, she buried her face in her hands. For what seemed like an eternity, the only sound in the room was her weeping.

Then, Betty said softly, 'I told you.'

'I'd have never believed it.' There was awe in Jed's voice. 'How do they get like this, these psychics? How can they know this stuff? Is it in them, like from the beginning? Are they born this way? Do they inherit it from their parents? Is this whole damned world a freak show?'

It's not a freak show! Karen screamed silently. *It's a wide, shining, beautiful place! I don't want to leave it – not now, when I've hardly started living! It's not fair! Ron and I haven't even had a chance yet! There are so many things that we both still have ahead of us!*

Though her eyes were closed tightly, she could see the dream-child shimmering before her. Like a carbon copy in miniature, she, too, had her small face covered with her hands. Her thin-boned, fragile fingers were shaped like Karen's. Her hair was the texture that Karen's had been in childhood.

If you're going to die, wailed the child, *I am never to be!*

The thought was so startling that it shocked Karen out of her tears. In that one split second, her third eye sprang violently open to its full capacity. In the yard at the front of the house, she saw people gathered. She saw the upraised fist that was aiming at the door.

She heard the sound of the knock before the blow fell.

'It's the police!' a voice shouted. 'Open that door and come out with your hands up!'

'Son of a bitch!' Jed exploded incredulously.

Whirling on his heel, he pointed the pistol at the closed door and pulled the trigger. The wood panel shattered with the close-range impact of the bullet.

Instantaneously, a second shot rang out, and Jed pitched forward. Betty screamed, and, in the playpen in the corner, Matthew let out a bellow of startled terror. As if on cue, the house was filled with the cries of frightened babies, wakened suddenly from drugged slumber.

It all of it happened too quickly for her to respond to.

Karen sat like a statue, incapable of intelligent reaction. As she stared at the uniformed man in the kitchen doorway, she found herself thinking inanely that she could never before have visualized an angel with a revolver in his hand.

21

As she descended the steps from the plane at the Albuquerque airport, Karen experienced a rush of fatigue that was so overwhelming that for a moment she thought she might need to request a wheelchair.

I'll never make it, she thought, as she measured with her eyes the distance that lay between the ramp and the terminal building.

Then she braced herself and started walking. It was almost over; she would not allow herself to fold up now.

The late-afternoon flight between Denver and Albuquerque had been a crowded one. On it, there had been the parents of most of the infants who had been recovered from the house in the mountains. Many of these people had flown to Denver just that morning. Others had managed to book flights the previous evening, after having received notification that their children had been found. Now, they were returning home with youngsters they had feared they would never see again, and the atmosphere in the plane had been one of such emotional intensity that the cabin had been filled with shrieks of wild laughter and outbursts of tears.

Once they had reached their cruising altitude, the pilot had put the controls on to automatic so he could walk through the cabin, offering congratulations. In the spirit of celebration, the stewardesses had distributed rattles to the rescued babies and served their mothers and fathers with complimentary cocktails.

Karen had sat next to Sue Wilson, who had spent the hour's flight time struggling to keep a rambunctious Matthew confined to her lap.

'He doesn't seem to have lost much energy,' she commented as the child squirmed and wriggled in an effort to climb over the seat back. 'He's come through this a darned sight better than his parents.'

Sue looked sunken-eyed and haggard, as though she had not slept for a week. Her husband, Steve, who had flown up with her that morning, had stayed over in Denver to drive Ron back when he was released from the hospital.

To the surprise of everyone, particularly Ron himself, the bullet that Jed had fired into his shoulder had not lodged there, but had passed straight through and ended up embedded in the trunk of a pine tree. The state police had managed to stop the bleeding before the arrival of the rescue squad, and Ron had then been transported to a hospital in Denver for a blood transfusion. He had been retained an extra day for observation.

'I should have stayed too,' Karen said now, as she and Sue walked together towards the gate. 'I could have come back with them and helped with the driving. My parents got so upset, though, when I tried to suggest it on the telephone that it just didn't seem worth the battle.'

'It's better you didn't anyway,' said Sue. 'Steve needs this time alone with Ron. They've got some things they need to work out between them. There's always been a distance there. I've never understood it.'

'I think it may be different now,' said Karen.

'I hope you're right. My husband's a workaholic. He doesn't get out and make friends the way he ought to, and he needs a brother to feel close to.' She shot Karen a quizzical glance. 'What's with *you* and Ron? Is there something special between you?'

'I don't know,' said Karen honestly.

The crowd at the gate was composed in a large part of relatives of the kidnapped children. Sue was immediately descended upon by an older couple who gave her a quick embrace and then swept Matthew out of her arms for a series of hugs and kisses. The man was tall and sandy-haired with a strong, high-boned face. The woman, when she raised her face to smile up at him, had eyes the colour of sapphires.

Karen heard her own name called, and turned to see her parents hurrying towards her. The reunion was an awkward one, stiff on one hand and overly emotional on the other.

Her mother reached her first and hugged her fiercely. Then, she released her and turned abruptly away.

Karen's father said, 'Now, Wanda, don't start crying again. She's home safe, and everything's fine now. I hope you realise, Karen, how much pain and worry you've caused. Your mother's a basket case. She can't handle this sort of pressure.'

'I'm sorry,' said Karen. 'I didn't have a choice.'

'That's a senseless statement,' said Mr Connors. 'You did have a choice, and you made it. You got a notion that you wanted to be a heroine, and you took off on an escapade that might have killed you. It wasn't even as though there were a need for it. The police had a handle on things.'

'No, they didn't,' Karen contradicted. 'There was a filing cabinet in that cabin that was filled with records of false adoptions that went back three years. The children had all been taken from other states, and the Colorado police hadn't been involved. They had no idea what was going on there.'

'Then how were they able to come to your rescue so conveniently?' her father asked her. 'The story was all written up in the morning paper. The police had that place staked out as though it were a war zone. They must have had it under observation.'

'They didn't know anything until yesterday morning,' Karen told him. 'They got an anonymous phone call informing them about everything. Dad, I'm so tired, I can't answer any more questions. Can we go home now?'

'Of course.' His expression changed abruptly from anger to deep concern. 'You are all right, aren't you, daughter? You weren't hurt in any way? On the phone, you said—'

'I wasn't hurt,' Karen assured him. 'I'm just tired.'

She and her mother waited together in front of the terminal building while Mr Connors brought the car up from the parking lot. Neither of them spoke. It was obvious that her mother was terribly upset. Aside from their initial embrace, she had not made any further gesture, nor had she tried to initiate conversation. Now, the two of them stood with space between them, as though they were strangers who had chanced upon each other in a public place and were waiting to share a car for convenience sake.

When the car arrived, Karen climbed into the back, and Mrs Connors got into the front seat beside her husband. Most of the way home, they drove in silence.

At one point, at a stoplight, Mr Connors glanced back at her to ask, 'How did Officer Wilson find that place in the mountains? Did *he* get a phone call also?'

'No,' said Karen. 'I told him where to go.'

She knew as she spoke that her father would not believe her. She also knew that he would not pursue the question, for he did not want to be forced to accept her answer.

She did not know which of her parents it was who shook her awake when they reached the house. She was conscious of hands on her shoulders and a voice speaking her name. Then, she was outside, crossing the lawn – entering through the front doorway – climbing the stairs to the second floor. Despite the weight of weariness that threatened to smother her, she kept moving on down the hall to its end.

When she entered her room, the half-filled suitcase still sat open on her bed, just as she had left it two days before. Too exhausted to face the prospect of putting the clothes away, Karen shoved the case off the side of the bed and watched its contents tumble out on to the rug.

The temptation to sink down on to the vacated mattress was almost irresistible. She knew, however, that this could not yet be allowed to happen.

With a tremendous effort of will, she turned away from

the beckoning bed and, as was her custom when under stress, crossed to stand at the window. In the world outside, the summer twilight was thick and golden as honey. Cicadas chanted in the trees in a drowsy, monotonous chorus. In the house next door, someone was playing the piano. The faint, silver tinkle trickled across the space between the houses and blended with the sounds of children playing in a neighbouring yard.

'All-y – all-y – in – free!' a young voice shrilled.

Hide-and-seek in the gathering dusk – a game of childhood.

In her own childhood, she had never been asked to play.

Karen Connors – seeker of missing children. I will play the game now as an adult for the rest of my life.

Time passed, and Karen waited. At last, she heard the footsteps she had been anticipating. They came clicking down the hall and stopped at the open doorway. There was a long moment of silence.

Her mother's voice spoke hesitantly. 'May I come in?'

Wordlessly, Karen nodded. The footsteps advanced into the room and muffled themselves in the bedroom carpet. The door closed with a gentle click.

Karen spoke without turning.

'Don't you think it's time that you told me the truth?'

'You already know it,' her mother said quietly. 'You've figured it out. You know I was the one who made the phone call to Denver. I realized the moment I discovered you'd left this house that you were heading into terrible danger.'

'You knew that, too, on the day the children were taken.' The pieces of the puzzle were starting to fall together, but the picture they were forming was one she would never have imagined. 'You were standing, folding laundry, when you had the vision. Why didn't you call the police and send them to the Tumbleweed?'

'I didn't know where it was,' her mother told her. 'It was all too foggy. I knew you were hurt and that you were in a kitchen. I thought, perhaps, it was the kitchen at the Centre. That's why I tried to phone you there.'

'How could you find me in another state when you couldn't right here?'

'I have no idea. I simply found that I could. I could see that location in my mind as clearly as though it were marked on a road map. I saw each turn of the road. I saw the house – the river – I could even see that dreadful dog. There's nothing logical about this gift of ours, Karen. I gave up trying to make sense out of it years ago.'

Now, Karen did turn. She regarded her mother incredulously.

'*Years ago?* Do you mean that you've *always* been a psychic?'

'I am *not* a psychic,' Mrs Connors said vehemently. 'I refuse to be classified that way. It's true, I was born with certain psychic abilities, but I've never made any attempt to develop and use them. I've hated them always. They made my childhood miserable. My schoolmates sensed I was different and I was left out of everything.'

'But, you've always told me how popular you were!' exclaimed Karen. 'You had so many friends! You were in all the school clubs! All the boys were in love with you!'

'That was how I wished my life could have been,' Mrs Connors said. 'It's what I've wanted for you. The truth of it is, I had no friends at all. I never went to parties or to dances. Boys were uncomfortable around me. The first date I ever had was with your father.'

'Your very first date was with *Dad*!'

'It was the spring I graduated from high school. Your father was doing accounting work for my father. He'd been over at the house all day, working on the income tax, and my mother invited him to stay on for dinner. Your dad was in his thirties and had never been married. He'd been too wrapped up in his work to develop a social life. He thought I was pretty, and I was. I looked a lot like you do now. He didn't sense that there was anything different about me. As you know, your father is not particularly perceptive.'

'You fell in love?' ventured Karen.

'It was love of a sort, but not the romantic kind. Your father was pleasant and kind, and my parents approved of him. I was afraid I might never have another opportunity to marry. I knew that I had to do something about finding a husband. You were waiting to be born.'

'I was – *waiting?*'

'I'd seen you in dreams,' her mother said matter-of-factly. 'You were there whenever my life was in any way threatened. The first time I saw you was in a fever dream. I had pneumonia, and the doctors were afraid that I wouldn't pull through. The second time was several years later. I was driving through an intersection, and suddenly, out of the blue, your face flashed in front of me. I was so startled that I instinctively hit the brake. An instant later, a car came barrelling through a stop sign. If I hadn't stopped when I did, I would have been killed. I can only speculate that on your part it was a form of self-preservation. If my life had ended before you were born, you could never have come into being.'

'Did you ever see other children?' Karen asked shakily. 'Did you see lost kids, the way I saw Bobby and Carla?'

'Yes, but they came in nightmares. My "black dreams", I used to call them, and they were horrible. For years I kept seeing them, those strange, frightened children who kept screaming to me to come to them. If I'd let them, they would have taken over my life. I held strong against them, though, and you can also. Except for these two recent instances when you were the one in danger, I haven't allowed myself a vision in almost thirteen years.'

'I don't think I can turn away like that,' said Karen.

'Haven't you listened to anything I've been saying?' Her mother's voice was sharp with exasperation. 'Don't you want marriage – children of your own – a normal life? No man wants to marry a freak, no matter how pretty she is. Look what happened to your relationship with Tim!'

She paused. When she spoke again, her tone was less strident.

'You have a chance to build a whole new image for yourself at college. You can meet somebody nice there and never let him find out about you. You can build yourself the same sort of happy life I have.'

'Mom,' Karen asked softly, 'are you really all that happy?'

'Well, of course,' said her mother.

'Then, why do you keep having migraines?'

'I'm headache prone. Lots of people have that problem. I've been having migraines since you were five years old.'

'Mom, I'm sorry,' said Karen. 'I know you want what you think is best for me, but I can't live my life the way you do yours. If, for some reason known only to God, I've been blessed with an extra eye, I'm going to learn how to use it as well as I can.'

'That vision I had thirteen years ago when you were five,' said her mother. 'That final vision – the one that made me close it all off.'

'Was it Mickey Duggin?'

Her mother nodded.

'You weren't the one who found him – I was. What followed after that was a total nightmare. Those letters and phone calls – the strangers ringing our doorbell – the people on our front lawn, trying to see in our windows – your father was simply horrified. The pressure it put on our marriage came close to destroying it.'

'It won't be like that for me,' Karen said with confidence. 'The man I marry will accept me for what I am.'

'I hope so,' her mother said softly. 'Oh, baby, I hope so!'

She reached out her hand and touched Karen's cheek.

The unfamiliar gesture, the gentleness of it – were so

much out of character that Karen could not answer her at all.

That night she dreamed again of the small blonde girl. The child was standing in a living room that was decorated in the same shades of blues and lavenders as Karen's current bedroom. Behind her, on a low bookcase, there stood a framed photograph of two women posed together on a stairway. The younger woman was dressed in a graduation gown. They had evidently been caught by the photographer at a moment at which they had not been expecting it, for the second woman was not looking into the camera lens. She had turned, instead, to gaze at the girl beside her, and on her face there was an expression of such pride and love that the intensity of it was almost unbearable to contemplate.

But it was the dream-child that Karen stared at in fascination.

My dear little daughter, who will your daddy be?

The girl raised her head. For the first time ever, Karen was able to see her eyes.

They were blue as a mountain lake.

Blue as the summer skies of Colorado.

They were the strange sort of brilliant heaven-sent blue that might run in one special family. As a dominant trait.

Lois Duncan
Stranger With My Face £1.95

For Laurie it had been a wonderful summer, filled with sun and sea. Perhaps the best summer of all her seventeen years . . .

Until the terror began to take over. First she had this chilling feeling that someone was watching her, even spying on her. Then Gordon, the boyfriend she was so proud of broke off with her. He'd seen her with another boy and Laurie insisted that it wasn't her. Then two of her friends started avoiding her because she'd said something that she knew she hadn't said!

What was happening to her? Was she going crazy? Or was something unbelievably sinister throwing a dark shadow across her golden summer skies . . .?

Merrill Joan Gerber
I'm Kissing As Fast As I Can £1.95

How many fathers actually *put* temptation in their son's path?

Sid's father Max decided to start a new life for himself after being widowed, and the move from Brooklyn to Los Angeles was only the first step. Max gained a medallion, lost weight, and tried everything new from karate to singles dances. He even tried to help his son's love life, telling him 'This is the age to sow your wild oats'.

Sid tried to keep up: the flesh was willing but the spirit was weak. But when Roshana turned up on his doorstep, a down-to-earth Brooklyn girl without false fingernails, Sid knew what he'd been waiting for . . .

Norma Klein
Beginner's Love £1.95

It was Joel's friend, Berger's idea to go to the Brooke Shields movie,
and it was Berger who made all the play for the two girls sitting in
front. It was also Berger who swapped phone numbers with them, but
it was Joel who Leda phoned just a few nights later.

Even before their first kiss on their first date at the theatre, Joel was
head over heels in love with Leda. He was seventeen and, compared
to Berger, he was really shy. Leda was just the way she was . . .

They shared so many first times together. So many that nothing would
ever be quite the same again for Joel. But then Leda missed her
period and something had gone wrong. Maybe everything was
suddenly going very wrong . . .

Rosemary Wells
When No One Was Looking £1.95

Tennis was Kathy's whole life. She had neither her younger sister
Jody's brains nor her best friend Julia's looks, but she did have a
phenomenal talent and there seemed no limit to what she might
achieve.

Everyone wanted Kathy to succeed. The mysterious and attractive
Oliver; her coach Marty because of the publicity should she become
famous; her parents because of the money and status success would
bring and Julia because . . . well perhaps because Kathy had once
saved her life. Only Jody was unsure.

For Kathy herself, winning became an obsession. Then one day she
lost a match she really should have won. That's when the doubts
started. And that's when someone decided to give Kathy a helping
hand – with tragic consequences . . .

All these books are available at your local bookshop or newsagent, or can be ordered direct from the publisher. Indicate the number of copies required and fill in the form below.

Send to: **CS Department, Pan Books Ltd., P.O. Box 40, Basingstoke, Hants. RG21 2YT.**

or phone: 0256 469551 (Ansaphone), quoting title, author and Credit Card number.

Please enclose a remittance* to the value of the cover price plus: 60p for the first book plus 30p per copy for each additional book ordered to a maximum charge of £2.40 to cover postage and packing.

*Payment may be made in sterling by UK personal cheque, postal order, sterling draft or international money order, made payable to Pan Books Ltd.

Alternatively by Barclaycard/Access:

Card No.

Signature:

Applicable only in the UK and Republic of Ireland.

While every effort is made to keep prices low, it is sometimes necessary to increase prices at short notice. Pan Books reserve the right to show on covers and charge new retail prices which may differ from those advertised in the text or elsewhere.

NAME AND ADDRESS IN BLOCK LETTERS PLEASE:

....

Name ——————————————————————

Address ————————————————————

——————————————————————

——————————————————————

——————————————————————

3/87